Lian Hearn's well-loved Tales of the Otori series, beginning with *Across the Nightingale Floor*, has sold over four million copies internationally. Her novel, *Blossoms and Shadows*, about life in Japan in the 1850s, also sold widely around the world. Lian has made many trips to Japan and has studied Japanese. She read Modern Languages at Oxford and worked as an editor and film critic in England before emigrating to Australia.

Visit Lian Hearn at facebook.com/lianhearnauthor
and www.lianhearn.com

the storyteller
and his three daughters

LIAN HEARN

First published in Australia and New Zealand in 2013
by Hachette Australia
(an imprint of Hachette Australia Pty Limited)
Level 17, 207 Kent Street, Sydney NSW 2000
www.hachette.com.au

This edition published in 2014

10 9 8 7 6 5 4 3 2 1

National Library of Australia
Cataloguing-in-Publication data:

Hearn, Lian.
The storyteller and his three daughters / Lian Hearn.

978 07336 3304 1 (pbk.)

A823.4

Cover design by Christabella Designs
Cover illustrations courtesy of Shutterstock
Cover illustration: Japanese nobleman stylised image. Created by Rapine, published in
Le Tour du Monde, Hachette, Paris, 1867
Text design by Bookhouse, Sydney
Typeset in Sabon by Bookhouse, Sydney
Printed and bound in Australia by Griffin Press, Adelaide, an Accredited ISO AS/NZS 14001:2009
Environmental Management System printer

In memory of my three fathers,
Tommy, Richard and John

I AM AKABANE SEI IX, professional storyteller. Over fifty years I have told countless stories, beginning as a child when I delighted my parents with my tales of mice, sparrows and so on and so on, but if I have any fame now it is as the author of 'The Silk Kimono'. Perhaps you have heard of this story. It began life ten years ago and was instantly popular; it had all the ingredients that appealed to an audience: love, jealousy, intrigue, betrayal. It was told first in one of those halls known as *yose*, designed for the intimate art of *rakugo*, fallen words or storytelling; then it was serialised in a Tokyo newspaper, and published as a book in countless editions. It has been undoubtedly my greatest success. But that success came after a long period when anxiety had robbed me of inspiration. I had many concerns – money, family, ageing – but what worried me most was the idea I might go blind like my father – I had various disturbances to my sight, flickerings and dark patches on the edge of my vision.

Of course blindness is no handicap to a storyteller, especially if like me and most of the Akabane family you are blessed with a phenomenal memory. My father performed despite his blindness for years. He, however, limited himself to traditional material whereas I needed something new, and that meant using my eyes to find it. Competition was growing fiercer every year. I had once been immensely popular, had filled the largest halls, had a huge following of fans and was universally known as Master, but early in 1884, the seventeenth year of Meiji, a *kinoe saru* or Monkey year, I became aware that something had changed. I was tired of my old stories, I felt my audiences were bored with them too, yet I seemed unable to produce anything new. At the same time a young Englishman appeared in the Tokyo *yose*, telling stories the like of which no one had heard before, ancient legends of sailors in search of a golden sheepskin and women whose faces turned men to stone, and sentimental modern tales of lost orphans, separated lovers and stolen inheritances.

I did not know the Englishman, Jack Green, but he had come to haunt me. My wife Tae, herself the daughter of a storyteller and a woman of blistering honesty, often went to his performances and developed something of a crush on him, which did not help: she never stopped talking about him and urging me to go and hear him. I did not want to and I dismissed the possibility that he might be any good – the idea was curiously painful – but finally my better self humbled me and, telling myself that even at my age with grown-up children

I might still learn and improve, I slipped unseen one day into the back of the hall. I hoped his Japanese would be poor, his gestures inappropriate, his story mundane, but I was captivated by the tale – an unusual and tragic story of a young French girl who led an army, was accused of witchcraft and burned to death – and by his manner of telling it. His Japanese was in fact perfectly fluent, with rare mistakes that only added an eccentric charm to his performance. I could tell he had a compassionate heart. In short he was wonderful.

I returned home deeply depressed.

I did not tell my wife where I had been but with her usual cunning she guessed. It was hard to keep anything from her. Our house was a comfortable size but all the rooms opened into each other and my study was next to the small room where we slept. Also after our long married life together she could interpret all my moods and silences.

Tae	You've been to see the Englishman? Isn't he every bit as good as I told you? Is that why you are so quiet and grumpy?
Sei	I hope I am not that mean spirited!
Tae	But you have to admit he's good!
Sei	Yes, he is very good.

I felt physically stabbed by my own words. My wife turned the blade.

Tae	And you're very jealous! Aren't his stories fresh and original? I am sure you are as good a storyteller but your material is so old and boring.

3

Jack Green's brilliance had instilled a rare humility in me and I had to admit, naturally only to myself, that my wife was right. I also feared my compassion had dried up over the years, though I was not going to share that with her either. I tried to console myself with thoughts of a philosophical nature: the stories were not mine or Jack Green's but belonged to the universe's constant cycle of creativity. What did it matter through which conduit they came? Arrogance and pride were the enemies of inspiration. Had my success and my self-satisfaction cut me off from my source?

But even while I was castigating myself and embracing the experience of being humbled, I was still wondering where I might find stories as strange and enthralling as Jack Green's. I could not plunder the wealth his European background gave him. I did not speak English or any other foreign language. I had never even really thought that the West might have its own tales and legends of such richness.

Before I lay down that night I sat in meditation for longer than usual, trying to clear my mind and praying for inspiration. A photograph of my father, taken in 1870, the year he died, stared at me, with his sad sightless eyes, from the shrine. I found myself envying him – not for his blindness but for dying when he did. He had seen the end of the era of the shoguns and the Restoration of 1868 that had ushered in the new government but had departed from this world before the upheavals and confusions of our modern time. I longed to return to his old Edo, as Tokyo used to be called, to a time before Jack Green was born, and then my mind began to wander and I found myself creating a whole life for the English boy. I saw him growing up in Yokohama, learning Japanese from the maids

4

and grooms and the children in the street, hanging round his father's office – an import–export business or perhaps an English-language newspaper. When I realised what my prayers had turned into I gave up and went to bed.

It was rather a cool night for June and had been raining most of the day. My wife complained of feeling cold and tried to crawl against me. I lay rigid without responding.

Tae	You could at least embrace me once in a while.
Sei	Really, we are a little old for that now!
Tae	You may be fifty but don't forget I'm six years younger. Is it that I don't appeal to you anymore?
Sei	It's nothing like that. I'm tired. Go to sleep.
Tae	What an unfeeling man you are! No wonder people aren't moved by your stories. You're incapable of emotion. It would serve you right if I looked for affection elsewhere!
Sei	Affection? What are you talking about?

I turned over and pretended to fall asleep. My wife was getting some strange ideas in her head. I blamed the magazines she read with their tales of romance and falling in love. Yet as always she had managed to wound me. I had become austere. I prided myself on it. It seemed at my age appropriate to seek the non-attachment of a buddha. But while I was disengaging myself from all emotion, audiences were demanding ever more emotional stories, filled with human passion and, shameful or not as it might be, a part of myself still wanted to give them that, to hold them spellbound and leave them thirsting for more.

I needed new material, that was clear. I resolved to make an effort. I would read more and I would keep a journal in which I would record all the ideas that came to me, the characters that inspired me. I would get to know their secrets and the passions of their lives. I became quite excited and could not sleep.

THE RAIN STOPPED during the night and the next day was muggy. My wife was already out when I woke and I got up slowly, rather tired after my restless night. My excitement had melted away: if anything I felt more jaded and dried out than ever.

Was it time for me to retire? I did not really entertain the thought seriously. My father had continued performing, even after he lost his sight, and died on stage from a seizure after a consummate rendering of 'The Revenge of the Soga Brothers' over ten consecutive days. That was the Akabane way and I hoped to follow him. Anyway, I could not afford to stop working. Supporting my various disciples, my daughters' marriages, the funerals of my parents and my wife's, and some unwise speculation by my manager had left me with heavy debts.

My wife came home from the market and began to prepare breakfast with the kind of deliberate clanging and banging that indicated she was in a bad temper. She always was lately, and I couldn't help blaming her for my lack of inspiration. I didn't speak to her, afraid of receiving some barbed reply, some implicit criticism, but I allowed myself a brief daydream of a different kind of life with a different kind of wife.

I sat on the edge of the back verandah overlooking the garden to eat, and before I had finished my manager, Kawata Rinjirō, dropped by to see if he should be hiring a hall for me before the end of the summer season or if I would consider doing a tour in the autumn. It was the second or third time he had called on us in a week; he was always somewhat embarrassed by the money he had lost, though I assured him I bore him no grudge at all, and he came up with many suggestions as to how I might earn it back.

He sat next to me and my wife banged a cup of tea down in front of him. I might have forgiven him but she always acted as if she never would – though her remarks from the previous night had remained in my mind and I began to wonder if she did not protest too much whenever Rinjirō came round. He was something of a womaniser and when I looked at Tae with fresh eyes I could see that she was still an attractive woman, with a trim figure and a bold gaze, looking not much older than our daughters.

Tae　　　　What's the use of ten halls or twenty tours if he has nothing to tell?

Rinjirō　　　　If that's the problem . . . well, Western stories

8

are popular at the moment. Perhaps the Master would try his hand at them?

Sei   I don't wish to seem to be copying or stealing from Jack Green.

Rinjirō   People have copied you in the past. Everyone steals from everyone else – they always have done. Storytellers are all thieves. They pilfer from old legends, history books, newspaper reports. Let me go ahead. Maybe the reality of some bookings will inspire you.

They were both staring hopefully at me. I thought of the pressure that would build up over the next few weeks, the mouth-drying, sleep-depriving terror of having nothing new to say, the humiliation of sitting on the stage in front of a sparse audience, delivering some well-worn story with banal gestures, watching half the spectators get to their feet and shuffle out before the end.

With another part of my mind I was imagining my wife and my manager having an affair. Maybe they had fallen hopelessly in love and were planning to murder me or drive me to suicide. The newspapers were full of stories about murderesses who plotted with their lovers to kill their husbands. Rinjirō was not a handsome man as such, but his skin was smooth, his hair thick and black, his nature lively and persuasive. He would be easily seduced if Tae turned her mind to it, despite his professed loyalty and admiration for me. These qualities would indeed add to the conflicts he would have to resolve. I would be the stock old fool, bamboozled by a younger wife . . . there were many woodblock prints on the subject and one of them floated into my mind, the foolish old man oblivious while a lusty youth pleasures his wife, his giant member poking through a hole in the screen.

Tae was looking at me shrewdly.

Tae   He's getting an idea. His eyes have glazed over and he's not really listening – both sure signs.

Rinjirō   So shall I book the hall, Master?

I took another piece of fish and Tae refilled my bowl with rice. As I ate slowly I imagined what it would be like if the food were poisoned, if the two people closest to me really did want to kill me. The thought filled me with such pain that my eyes grew hot. I tried to put my imaginings away, gripped by a superstitious fear that I would make them happen.

Sei   It was a fragment of an idea but it's not going to work. Don't do anything yet. I'll take the summer off and try to come up with some new ideas.

Rinjirō   I'll book a hall for the autumn. The Master back with brand-new material! I'm sure I'll be able to get some good advances.

Tae   We could certainly use that.

Rinjirō   I can let you have a little now – repayment, you know.

He took an envelope from the breast of his kimono and put it on the floor between us. I started to protest that there was no need but Tae quickly snatched it up and rushed off with it into the kitchen.

Rinjirō left. I took myself off to the privy without much success. I was blocked in more ways than one. I decided I would go for a walk; maybe the teeming city would give me some inspiration. We lived at that time in a rented place in Kyōbashi 2-chōme, not far from the kabuki theatre in Shintomi, next door to a lodging house also owned by our landlord, an extraordinarily fat and idle man named Hirano. As I was getting ready, Tae called from the kitchen.

Tae   Drop by next door. Hirano has a new lodger. He's been in France for years – he might have some interesting traveller's tales.

I did not reply. There was something extremely irritating about my wife's concern for my arid state. All the same, her words had planted some seed. The story I had heard Jack Green relate had come from France. Maybe I was being led in that direction . . . even though I knew nothing about France and didn't speak a word of French. I might very well do as she suggested but I would not give her the satisfaction of doing it right away.

Our dog, Aka, roused himself from his doze on the front steps and came with me, eyes bright in anticipation of adventures, ears pricked, tail curling over his back. He was a good dog, loyal, brave and cheerful with a useful ability to sense earthquakes seconds before we felt any tremors. He trotted behind me as I fell into the rhythm of walking, letting that daydreaming state which gives birth to ideas wash over me. I was alert to everything: two men arguing over a rickshaw fare, a young wife with a baby on her back, hurrying to

11

market with a few coins wrapped in a piece of paper, a blind street singer led to his place on the corner by a little boy, a dog crossing the road with an almost religious deliberation, miraculously avoiding handcarts and horse-drawn trams. It was a commonplace to say everyone had a story worth telling, but the idea of relating any of them filled me with a mixture of boredom and revulsion, and I tried not to look at the blind man in case his affliction might be catching.

Aka wanted to follow the single-minded dog but I called him back and told him to go home. He looked at me for a moment but then obeyed. I watched him amble down the street and wondered what it would be like to see the world through a dog's eyes. I thought of Bakin's wildly popular story of the Eight Dog Warriors, which I had so loved when I was young for the heroism and bonds of friendship it depicted. Could I attempt something like that? Or a modern story, Aka's account of his life with our family: 'I Am a Dog'? The trouble was I was no Bakin, but nor was I truly modern. I was stuck between past and future.

My wanderings led me through Ginza, around the gardens of what was now the Imperial Palace, to Nihonbashi. It was getting very hot so I stopped under the willow trees beside the river for a bowl of cold soba and some barley tea. As often happens, I was recognised; the owner of the stall professed himself a great fan and asked where I was performing. When I replied that I was resting over the summer, he told me he had heard a rumour that I had retired.

I corrected him quite sharply; I was preparing a new story, I said. He then regaled me with glowing reports of various recent performances he had attended, some by my fellow Guild members and, naturally, Jack Green. I nodded affably while my guts churned and a good meal was ruined.

Sobaya-san Have you heard the Englishman tell the history of the French Revolution?

Sei Hmm.

Sobaya-san All those beheadings! Gruesome! The French even invented a special decapitation machine – quick, efficient and painless. Those Westerners – the ideas they come up with!

Sei Hmm.

There it was again: another little push towards France. I decided I would now follow my wife's advice and pay a visit to Hirano's new lodger.

Hirano Bimyō was a mysterious fellow. As I said, he was fat and idle and he never seemed to go out but he had a number of shady acquaintances who kept him informed about everything that happened in the city. I used to think of him as a huge old octopus with many fish darting around him, not a few of them sharks. His room, to which his wife, Chie, directed me, had an underwater feel to it, being dark, greenish and smelling of Hirano's distinctive odour, which was slightly marine.

Chie was a cousin of my wife and like her was in a permanent state of exasperation with her husband. She expressed it not by clanging the cooking pots but by showing her superiority in everything she did.

Hirano was sprawled on the tatami by the open door, fanning himself and dabbing at his sweaty face with a handtowel. The little garden was dense with greenery, the colour broken by one very fine scarlet azalea. Petals floated on the stone basin, filled by last night's rain, and an insect was chirping. Both this house and mine were former merchants' dwellings which Hirano had snapped up around 1866, shortly before the overthrow of the last of the Tokugawa shoguns, who had ruled Japan for two hundred and fifty years. When the lords, their samurai and their families went home to their provincial domains, Edo emptied overnight, property values plummeted and many shop owners lost everything. The houses retained little pockets of their former luxury: hidden gardens, spacious entrance halls with stone steps, cypress wood verandahs, though Hirano had converted his into as many separate rooms as possible for his lodgers.

He greeted me as usual with the excessive friendliness that made me distrust him. Talking to him I always felt I was jumping and dodging like a ninja in a kabuki play. It was hard to believe he simply lay there unmoving while I was going through the experience of wrestling with an agile and slippery opponent. Added to this he was my landlord and I owed him money – several months of rent to be exact. He never mentioned this but neither of us ever forgot it.

There was a tray on the floor next to him holding a flask of sake and some cups. He poured one for me and we drank together. I was not a great drinker; it upset my stomach, made my face turn red and left me with vicious hangovers, but I never refused a drink from Hirano. I had not realised there was anyone else in the room until Hirano spoke over his shoulder and a man I knew slightly, Ushiwa Teiji, shuffled forward out of the gloom.

Ushiwa was one of those ruffians who swaggered around the streets of Tokyo getting into trouble, baiting the police, insulting foreigners and so on. Many of them described themselves as *sōshi*, stalwart youths, recalling the men of high purpose, the *shishi*, of the previous generation. I found these young men quite entertaining. Some supported the liberals and the People's Rights Movement while others were hard conservatives and were often employed by the police to break up the progressives' meetings. Most often the *sōshi* ended up fighting each other – a good brawl seemed to be what both sides really wanted.

True to type Ushiwa had a black eye and a split lip, wounds he bore with all the pride of an old warrior. Not that he was from the former samurai class, although a few *sōshi* were; he was, more typically, a farmer's son, unemployed, estranged from his family and far from his home town. He affected the *sōshi*'s supposedly manly style of dress, dishevelled and rough, his hair unkempt. *Sōshi* pretended to despise women and formed close, almost erotic, bonds with each other as comrades and brothers-in-arms. There were stories there, I was sure of it, set in the Satsuma Rebellion perhaps or back in the battle of Ueno, or maybe this most recent confrontation in Gunma, which Ushiwa described at some length.

Ushiwa   You should dramatise it, Master. I could give you all the details and the background. You could be a great help to our cause.

Sei   What is your cause exactly?

Ushiwa   Democracy, of course! People's Rights! No taxation, no conscription, freedom and justice.

Hirano   Plenty of fighting.

Sei   It's probably cowardly of me but I always avoid politics. It's against regulations, you know.

Hirano   The Master doesn't want to end up being closed down.

Sei   Speaking of democracy, I hear you have a new guest recently returned from France.

Hirano   So my wife tells me. I haven't met him yet. You know she handles all these things. Shall we get him over? We'd all like to talk to him, I expect.

Hirano reached out and struck the brass bowl next to him several times. Its clear notes reverberated through the garden and along the verandah. We all fell silent, listening for a response. From the main house came the sound of some disturbance; someone was retching violently and crying out in a voice that sounded feverish, full of anxiety and fear. Chie could be heard alternately soothing and shouting. A slight frown puckered Hirano's smooth baby-like face and he struck the bowl again more forcefully.

After a few moments his wife came hurrying along the verandah.

Chie   What do you want? I can't help you right now. The Korean boy is sick. I've never seen anything like it – he's burning up and streaming from both ends!

Hirano   Cholera! Get him out of here. The quarantine patrol will be going past any moment. Get them to take him away!

Chie   I don't think it's cholera. He says it's food

17

poisoning. He ate tainted carp last night, he says. Give him a day or two.

Hirano   Get him out of my house now!

He poured sake and drank two cups straight off, pressed more on Ushiwa and myself and told us to drink up quickly and leave. I had never seen him so agitated. He had turned pale and was sweating even more heavily. Could my octopus be a hypochondriac? Of course, cholera was a terrifying illness and there had been many cases that summer. Isolation was the only way of controlling it and quarantine patrols were in the streets every day. Sake, incidentally, was meant to be both prevention and cure.

Ushiwa observed that it was much more likely to be food poisoning and did not budge. *Sōshi* were afraid of nothing, not even cholera. I said I would come back another time and went to the front of the house to see what was happening.

My sense of smell had always been extremely acute – something of a burden in a large city like Tokyo. As I walked through the entrance hall I caught a whiff of vomit and excrement which turned my already queasy stomach. Outside the air was hardly any fresher. The quarantine patrol, which at that time went past every afternoon, had halted in front of the house. Two policemen, two hygiene inspectors, and some porters pulling a cart, were surrounded by a small crowd who, despite the dangers of the disease, did not want their relatives taken away to isolation centres where, it was rumoured, doctors with long noses like goblins extracted their organs and sold them for medicine.

Aka had left his usual position by my front door and was circling the police, barking. I seized him by the scruff and made him be quiet. There was a great deal of yelling, sobbing, grabbing and shoving going on and the police were preparing to crack a few heads and break a few fingers with their clubs.

The porters were half-naked and had cloths wrapped around their faces so only their eyes were visible. Devoid of any human expression, they looked like demons from hell. Two of them ran past me into the lodging house, leaving a distinctive smell of disinfectant and ash in their wake.

There were three or four sick people already in the cart. I noticed the efforts that had been made for them: quilts to lie on (quite a sacrifice for they would surely be burned), a flask of tea, a damp towel, a piece of fruit, and the usual talismans against disease – amulets and scarlet-coloured pictures, of the god of medicine, no doubt, subduing the cholera demon. No one could fail to be moved by such a sight. Truly, I told myself, the nature of existence is suffering.

I did not know who 'the Korean boy' was and I regret to say I had already formed a somewhat negative image in my head, based on nothing in particular, for I had never knowingly met a Korean at that time, although there were a few in Tokyo who had fled their oppressive regime hoping for a better life. So when the porters emerged carrying between them a half-conscious young man of striking beauty, I did not immediately realise that this was Chie's Korean lodger. He could not have been more than seventeen or eighteen years old, with white skin made almost translucent by fever, and slender limbs. His lips were startlingly red in his pale face and his hair was long and silky.

Unaffected by his looks, the porters placed him none too gently in the cart. Apart from Chie, who was standing in the

front entrance biting her lip and wringing her hands, he seemed
to have nobody who cared if he lived or died.

However, just as the porters were preparing to lift the
handles and move off, someone came swiftly from across the
street and spoke to the hygiene officials. It was a man I knew
slightly. I had met him at Hirano's and in other places in the
neighbourhood. Occasionally I saw him in the bathhouse. His
name was Yamagishi Takayuki. At first I'd placed him as just
another *sōshi*, though at the opposite end of the spectrum to
Ushiwa Teiji. But there was a lot more to him than that. Once
I'd seen him coming out of an old house, much grander than
my own, in Tsukiji, which was a short distance away near the
river, and Chie told me he lived there, alone, apart from the
servants. I'd imagined his background – a former samurai from
one of the south-western domains, now struggling to make a
new life in Tokyo, nostalgic for the old feudal days. He always
wore traditional clothes and there was something old-fashioned
about him, a sense of entitlement perhaps and a concern for
personal honour. According to Chie, who had more than a soft
spot for him, he was from Chōshū, his wife was dead, and he
made his living from gambling, on cards and on horses. He
often walked past and occasionally called in on her.

He had a mysterious, unmistakable authority. People did
what he told them to do and took pains not to cross him.
I concluded that he had powerful connections, though I had
no idea what they might be. We did not run into each other
often but when we did I made sure I was polite.

Now Yamagishi exercised this authority on the officials.
They stood back and let him approach the cart, watching as
he lifted the Korean boy and held him against his chest. The

boy clung to him, half-delirious, calling out something about horses and tigers, wild beasts roaming in his inflamed brain. Yamagishi soothed him, speaking his name, *Kyu, Kyu*. It had a calming sound like a dove.

One of the policeman stepped forward to remonstrate but at the same moment a young woman came out of the crowd and announced in a clear voice that in her opinion he did not have cholera.

Again I knew who she was. She lodged with Chie and helped her with meals and housework. Unlikely though it seemed, she was a medical student, probably one of only three or four at that time in Tokyo – women, I mean. There were any number of male students. Medicine offered a lucrative career and now doctors had to be licensed they had a much higher social standing than in the old days.

Itasaki Michi was small in stature and rather doll-like. She wore a divided skirt and a severe short jacket; her hair was pulled back in the plainest of styles, yet none of this could hide how attractive she was, with her oval face, clearly defined eyebrows and delicate ears like a child's. You would not expect her to be living alone in Tokyo pursuing a career like a man. Universities, like high schools, were all-male domains, tight knit, exclusive and misogynistic. It was hard to imagine a young woman lasting half a day in that environment. Taunting and hazing would be ongoing; physical attacks were not unknown. Yet I fancied I had observed in her, the few times I had spoken to her, something hard and unfeminine: ambition, indifference to the opinion of others, and fearlessness.

When my wife read out accounts in the newspapers of 'poison women' who seduced men and then murdered them,

Miss Itasaki's features always came into my mind. I was a little fascinated by her already but now her presence hit me like a bolt of lightning.

Yamagishi and Miss Itasaki looked at each other for an instant, then Yamagishi made a slight beckoning gesture with his head and turned towards the house. Miss Itasaki followed him, hoisting her leather satchel up on her shoulder.

I was still feeling queasy and the sake must have gone to my head, for the scene before me suddenly took on a profound significance. I was fairly sure Yamagishi and Miss Itasaki had never met before but I thought I sensed an immediate erotic charge between them. The man and the boy had obviously been lovers; the man and the woman would be before long.

The officials moved away, the crowd gradually dispersed and I entered my house, told Tae to bring me green tea, went straight to my study and began to write.

I DECIDED I WOULD start with the man and the boy, with Yamagishi Takayuki and Kyu, and I realised I would have to tackle the delicate subject of *nanshoku* or male love. I found myself reflecting on why the subject had become so delicate in recent times. For centuries *nanshoku* had been a staple, in one form or another, of warrior tales: an older man takes a young lover, educates and guides him, both are inspired to greater feats of martial arts and military glory, they die in each other's arms on the battlefield and so on and so on. It was an essential part of samurai culture, more admirable and more erotic than falling in love with a woman, which had something rather weak and common about it.

It came as a shock to discover Westerners had a different attitude, disapproving strongly with their public face, whatever their private preferences might be. Our leaders hastened to pass laws to prove we were a civilised nation and male love became for a short time illegal. It was no longer strictly so, I believed, but the official censure remained, which meant I would have to tread carefully. Of course, human nature is such that nothing is more attractive than the forbidden. Many refused to give up *nanshoku* out of loyalty to the past and to tradition, while others were led to try it, out of a taste for the illicit. In the kabuki theatre male love continued to flourish as it always had, and as I would find out.

Priests and their acolytes also figured in many old stories of male love. In my experience it was unusual not to feel a certain erotic affection in the master–disciple relationship. There were powerful elements of submission and dominance, admiration, hero worship and power. Pupils worked harder and learned faster. Masters were more tender and more patient. I'd found, though, that it was safer to leave all this in the realm of the unspoken and the unrealised. If my disciples fell in love with me I used that to make their work better, while remaining physically distant. But humans are passionate creatures and they fall in love helplessly, men with boys, boys with girls, women with men, men with women, and without that my stories would be boring.

However, to avoid censorship and disapproval I had to adjust my tales and I could see that *nanshoku* was going to require some tact. I would have to present it subtly so that the authorities were not offended but not so subtly that my audience did not catch what I was talking about.

I was about to start describing how Kyu and Yamagishi met and was mulling over a few preliminaries:

- Was it in Korea or Japan? Could be either.
- How did the boy get to Japan? No idea.
- What did I know about Korea? Not much.

My mind drifted back to the past and to the passionate admiration I had felt as a teenager for one of my father's disciples, how I had imitated his speech, the way he held his fan, how thrilled I was if he noticed me or spoke to me. Could I retrieve from that the emotions Kyu might hold for Yamagishi Takayuki?

From that moment I began to think of him by his given name of Takayuki. He became a character for me and so I felt I knew him intimately. At the same time I decided I would call Miss Itasaki Michi. There was something rather thrilling merely in linking their names in this familiar fashion.

I took another gulp of green tea hoping to get my imagination going and then our dog began to yelp excitedly in the way he only did for a member of the family, and I heard a voice call out from the entrance. I recognised it as my youngest daughter's and my heart sank. I loved this girl, Shigure; even though she was our third disappointment, she had always aroused in me feelings of utmost tenderness. She was my favourite out of our three girls but she had also caused me the greatest anxieties. She had been followed by the child I never talked about, our son for whom Tae put flowers in the shrine and cooked special food every year on the anniversary of his death.

Even now Shigure was a grown-up and had been married for a year, each time I saw her I became so concerned for her I could not write. Her health had always seemed poor but she had survived childhood and been content at home. It had been painful when she married and moved away and I knew she was not happy, which depressed me.

The marriage had been arranged with a young man, Ono Renzō, who was a clerk with a lawyer in Yokohama. It was a good position with prospects; he was ambitious in the modern fashion and was about to qualify as a lawyer himself. He was also becoming wealthy, having a flair for buying and selling land. I had not yet asked him for a loan but the idea was always at the back of my mind. There was something comforting about having a son-in-law with assets.

It was late in the day, an unusual time for a purely social visit. I immediately suspected something was wrong. The ink had dried on my brush; I poured a little more water on the inkstone and began again.

When I write I hear my own voice inside my head, performing the story. Sometimes I even speak it out loud. I write down my scripts and work and rework them. They may sound improvised and natural when I am on stage but they are the result of hours of labour. In the first instance, however, if all is going well, all I have to do is listen. I was hoping to hear Kyu's voice tell me his life story but what in fact hit my ears was a shriek from downstairs, followed by a slap and then wild sobbing.

I laid down my brush and got to my feet with a sigh. Obviously there would be no more writing this evening.

When I went into the living room I fell over a large bundle dropped on the floor by my daughter; it looked as though she had brought clothes for a lengthy stay, most of her possessions and something solid, like a book or a slab of paper.

Shigure was crouched, crying and shaking, next to the kitchen while my wife shouted at her, our dinner burning in the pan.

Sei   What on earth?

Tae   She says she's left her husband.

Sei   That's not possible!

Shigure   It is! I have! And I am never going back!

Tae   Of course you are! First thing in the morning. I'll drag you there myself.

Shigure   Then I'll run away tonight. I'll sell myself on the streets or drown myself in the river.

Sei   Calm down! Tell us what happened.

Shigure   Nothing happened. He's boring. He chews with his mouth open. He wants to – you know – every night!

Tae   Yes, yes, and his farts smell and his toenails are dirty: he's a man. You may as well get used to it. And make the most of the night. The time will come when he won't want to touch you at all.

I took a quick look at my toenails, which were a little dirty after my long walk through the city.

Shigure   I don't love him. Anyway, I don't want to be married to anyone. I want to write novels.

Sei   This is your mother's fault. She should never have brought those worthless magazines into the house.

Tae   My fault? Am I the storyteller in the family? Oh, no, it's your fault. She gets it from you.

Shigure   Father, I can write stories, just like the ones in the magazines. I've written one. I'm going to submit it.

Tae   Where is it? Give it to me!

Shigure   You want to read it, Mother?

Tae   No, I need something to stoke up the fire now dinner is ruined and I will have to start all over again.

My wife was about to go through Shigure's bundle but I prevented her. My shortcomings might have been many but my respect for the story was absolute. For me the story was Emperor and we were all its subjects. It was greater than us; we had to unite to serve it or our little realm would fall into anarchy. I was not really a traditionalist. I saw nothing wrong with female storytellers; some of them were really quite good. I would not have been unhappy if one of my girls had taken over my cushion and my fan. As it happened, the older ones had the personality but not the imagination, while Shigure had never lacked imagination but was too shy to perform in public. But if she had found another outlet I could not stand in her way and I certainly could not let her work be destroyed.

At the same time I was now in something of a dilemma. Divorce was not uncommon, in fact it happened all the time, but it would be insulting to Renzō to allow my daughter to come home and I would have to abandon my hopes of a loan. And if they did get divorced, to start looking for another husband after all the difficulties I'd had marrying off three daughters – well, it was a discouraging prospect.

I said Shigure could stay for one night. Tae objected that Renzō would be worrying about her, and Shigure explained she had told him I was not well and she was coming home to look after me for a few days.

Oh story! Your realm is falsehood and we all tell lies in your service!

My wife, in a very bad temper, salvaged what she could of the meal; we ate in silence and went to bed.

IN THE NIGHT I remembered Hirano's guest from France whom I had been about to meet, and since the atmosphere in my own house was no better the next morning, after a dismal breakfast, I went next door. Most of the lodgers had already left but the French fellow, as I called him, was still there eating in a corner, and so to my delight was Michi, cleaning up in her usual brisk and efficient way.

Sei   How is the young man? Is he better?

Michi   I sat up most of the night with him. The fever broke and he was well enough to get up this morning and go to the theatre.

Sei   He is an actor?

Chie   He wants to be an actor. In the meantime he

works down in hell in the Shintomi-za, not even a proper stagehand. Imagine how hot it will be there today!

Sei   So it was not cholera?

Michi   Just food poisoning, as I thought.

She removed her apron, untied the cords that held back her sleeves and handed them to Chie.

Michi   I must go now. I've got a lecture. I'll see you this afternoon.

Chie   You should give up. You look exhausted. What sort of life is this for a young woman? You should be home with your family.

Michi   I'm not ready to give up yet. I'll be all right.

She smiled, made a small bow to me and went towards the back of the house. A few moments later she came out, carrying her satchel, slipped into her wooden clogs and called goodbye.

I had a mind to walk with her wherever she was going but I also wanted to talk to my French fellow. Chie decided for me; after grumbling quietly about Michi, she took me forward and introduced me to Okuda Satoshi, making me blush a little at her fulsome description of me, which Okuda listened to with a grave ironic expression as though seeing straight through her flattery.

He was in his late twenties, a thin man, a little over average height, I guessed, though I couldn't be sure as he was sitting down. He was dressed in Western clothes which I assumed he had bought in France – they were of better material and cut than anything available in Tokyo – and he looked like a typical

31

intellectual with his high forehead, wire-rimmed glasses and gleaming eyes.

Chie offered to bring me something to eat and I accepted. I mentioned before that her reaction to her indolent husband was somewhat different from my wife's to me. She had long been engaged in a complex battle of wills with him which required her to excel in everything she did. She was a wonderful cook and the food was always superb. I could not imagine why she should be so good to him, when suddenly Hokusai's picture of the fisherman's wife's dream came into my mind, the lecherous octopus's tentacles reaching into the woman's hidden places. My face grew rather hot and I could not bring myself to look at her. I was fond of erotic prints, *shunga*, but they had a habit of appearing in my mind at inopportune moments.

Okuda made a comment about the 'maid' and I was able to enlighten him, giving myself a taste of that small vicarious pleasure we experience when we reveal someone of our acquaintance to be more interesting or cleverer than was suspected. His eyes lit up even more when he learned Michi was a medical student.

Aha! He likes her! Another triangle! I put that thought, and the Hiranos' sex life, away for future use and started to question him about life in France.

I discovered to my great pleasure that Satoshi (now I knew he was going to become a character I felt free to think of him by his given name) loved reading, not only philosophy and politics but also novels and poetry. We talked for about half an hour and then he took out a watch and jumped to his feet (yes, he was tall), explaining that he was going for an interview for a position with a foreign languages academy.

We made an arrangement to meet again, and with my head buzzing with new names – Victor Hugo, Guy de Maupassant, Charles Baudelaire – I walked down towards Shintomi. I had decided to go to the theatre. I wanted to find out how a Korean boy had ended up a theatre rat.

Kabuki had gone through some difficult times in the last twenty years – audiences dwindling, plays relying more on stagecraft than on human emotions and great writing, actors who were all show but hollow inside. It was criticised for being old-fashioned and incomprehensible, and for a while it seemed kabuki might go the way of the two swords and the topknot, but it had always been a cunning and shameless art and it soon found itself in bed with the right people again. Now it was in a golden era. Some minister or other had decided it was not a relic of the feudal past after all but a genuine expression of national identity which deserved encouragement and patronage. Audiences were turning to it in search of reassurance in a world that seemed to be reshaping itself every night so you woke up in the morning to find a red brick bank where your favourite eating place had been the day before, or the route you had been taking for years across the city had been cut in half by gleaming railway tracks. And, perhaps most importantly, our three great actors were in their prime. All from old kabuki families, they had become the idols of the city, each commanding hundreds of devoted followers. Two of them, Kigawa Sakutarō and Nishiyama Kenjirō, were the stars of the Shintomi-za, while the third held sway at a theatre closer to Kanda.

My oldest daughter, Yuri, was married to the stage manager of the Shintomi-za, Furuda Katsuhiro, but despite this family connection I did not go to the theatre often, nor did I see much of Furuda. He was at the theatre day and night and during the summer break liked to go away into the mountains and conquer one peak after another. I suppose in his job he had become addicted to life on the edge. It took an unusual mixture of brutality and sensitivity to launch the great ship that is a play and keep it on course, and Yuri did not see much of her husband either, though he had somehow found the time to give her two sons and she seemed content with that.

The reasons I did not go to the theatre were complex and I did not completely understand them myself. I had devoted my life to storytelling with no props, not even music, just the narrator, holding a fan and a handtowel, sitting on a cushion in front of the audience. It was my voice alone that created the world and its characters and guided them through birth and death and laughter and love and loss and warfare. In kabuki, in contrast, great efforts were made to represent reality. Snow and rain fell from the heavens, mist rose from the ground, fires flickered, arrows quivered in bodies, blood spurted from wounds, severed heads fell with a thud, animals – horses, tigers, deer, cats, foxes, even frogs – trotted, prowled and jumped in a convincingly lifelike way. The audience gave themselves over to belief in the mimicry but what happened on stage was no more real than what happened within the words of my stories. In fact it was less real, in my opinion, until it became too real when the audience got drenched or the theatre caught on fire.

The outside of the Shintomi theatre was decorated with red lanterns and signs and posters advertising the names of the performers. There was quite a crowd and I was not sure I would get in but someone must have recognised me for a young man approached me and, addressing me as Master, handed me a wooden ticket tag and took me to the head of the line. I have to admit it was gratifying – among the crowds holding woodblock prints of their favourite actors and sighing *Sakutarō, Kenjirō!* – and I took my seat and accepted the offer of some tea and a lunch box in a pleasant frame of mind.

The play was *Osaka Castle* – a new historical piece about the fall of the castle in 1615 and the suicide of Hideyoshi's widow and their son, his heir, Toyotomi Hideyori. During the long years of the Tokugawa rule, which the 1868 Restoration brought to an end, this portrayal of what might be interpreted as a lack of loyalty on the part of the regime's founder, Ieyasu, could not have been performed. The name of Toyotomi Hideyoshi, the great unifier of the sixteenth century, was never uttered on stage. Pseudonyms were invented for him and his generals but, even with this disguise, accounts of his life came under careful scrutiny by the government and were often heavily censored or banned outright. Now things had been reversed; the current government sought to portray the dynasty they had replaced as enemies of the Emperor – backward, feudal lords who had kept Japan in darkness all those years while the rest of the world (that is, the West) was embracing renaissance, enlightenment, revolution and progress. Toyotomi Hideyoshi was now the epitome of loyalty and courage, while the tragic fate of his son was being newly discovered.

I munched on parched nuts while reflecting on all this and waiting for the play to begin. The Shintomi-za did not have electric light at that time and performances were held during the day, lit by the high windows around the theatre. People came and went during the early scenes but once the story got underway they settled down and it was easier to concentrate. I could not deny that there were moments in kabuki that knocked the breath out of your body and *Osaka Castle* had at least two of these: Kenjirō's first entrance as Ieyasu and the final stage revolve that revealed the ruined castle, while Ieyasu, magnanimous in victory, lamented the end of the Toyotomi. At these moments the audience went completely quiet as the spell of theatre fell over them.

The role of Hideyori was played by Sakutarō. He had a flair for portraying doomed heroes and as usual he did it well, though I was not so impressed by his exit through the trapdoor. Trapdoors really were a little too mechanical for my taste and he was a heavy man; the whole floor shook as he dropped through.

At lunchtime my son-in-law himself brought me my lunch box, thanked me for coming, inquired after my health and my wife's and so on and so on. He was a small wiry man with a very youthful air and was known in the theatre as Kat'chan. I asked if he could meet me afterwards and he agreed, saying the play was in its last weeks and could virtually run itself. He would return to the theatre later to check everything was in place for the next day's performance and to close up.

We went to a nearby teahouse, talked about the play and briefly about my grandsons. Then I broached the subject I was interested in.

Sei   I heard you have a young Korean working for you. Unusual, isn't it?

Kat'chan   It's strange you should mention him. I was about to fire him today. He's meant to help Sakutarō at the trap; he fumbled it and Sakutarō landed badly – he could have broken a leg. Then the kid fainted during the revolve. He was lucky not to get caught under the wheels as the stage turned. I've seen men crushed like that. You should come and see what goes on backstage and underneath, Master. It's chaos. Everything on stage looks so beautiful and so perfect. Down below it's as hot as hell and my men work like slaves in a silver mine.

Sei   You said, 'about to fire him'?

Kat'chan   Sakutarō persuaded me not to. He must have noticed how the boy looks when he almost fell at the trap – it's hard to believe he hadn't before but he is extraordinarily self-absorbed even for an actor. I didn't want to take the Korean on; first, precisely because he's Korean and that's bound to get out, even though he uses a Japanese name, Maeda Kyuichi – everyone just calls him Kyu – and second, he's a little too beautiful. I thought he was bound to cause problems, but I was put under some pressure to hire him.

Sei   By whom?

Kat'chan   Kobayashi, the theatre owner. When I refused, a couple of persuasive thugs – you know, *tattoos* – took to following me home, but who was behind them I don't know and Kobayashi won't tell me. I suppose Kyu's got some powerful lover who wants to indulge his passion for theatre or . . .

Sei   Or?

Kat'chan   Or he's some kind of informant. Though who he could be spying on in the bowels of the Shintomi-za I have no idea. There's no time for idle chat down there and anyway they're all just theatre rats.

Sei   So what about Sakutarō?

Kat'chan   He sent for him after the performance today, and has now told me he wants him on stage in black as his assistant in the next production.

Sei   That's quite a promotion.

Kat'chan   Sakutarō says his present assistant is getting too old, so I've got to find him a position in the office and Kyu will take his place. These actors have become so demanding. They think they're gods. And it's always me who has to try to keep them happy. It's a nightmare. But I'll tell you something else interesting: the next play is to be about Hideyoshi's invasion of Korea and the rival generals, Konishi Yukinaga and Katō Kiyomasa – another special request from someone whose name is kept from me. You know what I think? I think someone behind the scenes wants the Korean question back on the agenda. Someone wants the public to get the idea that Japan should take over Korea. Isn't it a strange coincidence that we should be asked to employ a Korean who can pass as Japanese, and present a new play on Korea? What do you think it means, Master?

I could think of several possible narratives; in fact my head was buzzing with ideas, but I did not want to pick a definitive one yet so I simply shrugged and widened my eyes to convey astonishment. At that moment the actors burst into the teahouse like a flock of exotic birds; a gaggle of fans trying to follow them was shooed away by the doorman. Sakutarō had his hand on the back of Kyu's neck and I could tell from the casual sensuality of the gesture and the proud, vulnerable expression on the boy's face that they were already lovers.

IT HAD BEEN a long day. I was looking forward to a visit to the bathhouse and some dinner, but when I got home another family drama had erupted. My second daughter, Teru, was now crying in the kitchen. My wife was not shouting at her or slapping her. She was comforting her and when I came in gave me a furious look as though whatever had happened was all my fault.

If Shigure was my favourite, Teru was my wife's. They were alike in looks and character, and in our family squabbles they were usually in one camp, Shigure and I in the other, while our oldest, Yuri, tried to act as arbiter and peacemaker. Teru had married one of my disciples, Kojima Tensa, and they lived not far away with his widowed mother. Tensa had the makings of a great comic performer. He had an expressive, mobile face with rather large eyes, and a voice of unusual clarity and fluency.

He could deliver a tale faster than anyone else alive, had a gift for spontaneous wordplay, and possessed that indefinable sense of one's own presence that all the top storytellers have. It takes courage and assurance to face an audience and hold their attention hour after hour, sometimes day after day. I liked to think my son-in-law's talents were somehow thanks to my teaching, but the truth is he was born with them.

Tensa liked music and had a good singing voice. He often worked with a young musician, Maruoka Yūdai, and they had recently completed a very successful tour of the Kansai area.

I asked with some trepidation what had happened but Teru sobbed even louder and ran past me into the living room. Tae pulled me into the kitchen and started whispering at me.

Tae   Don't tell me you didn't know?

Sei   Know? Know what? What are you accusing me of now?

Tae   That Tensa was a – you know . . .

Sei   I have no idea what you are talking about.

Tae   An *okama*! He doesn't like women. She found him in bed with the musician. She says he hasn't touched her since the wedding night, when he was too drunk to do much. No wonder there are no children. His mother blames her, says she's driven him away into Yūdai's arms and any proper woman would know how to kindle a man's desires. But he's fallen in love with Yūdai. That's why they go away together on tour so often.

I could not really say anything because I had known about Tensa's leanings. He had watched my other disciples a little too ardently and had shown signs of having a crush on me when he was younger, helping me put on my sandals or my jacket, scrubbing my back in the bathhouse. A hundred years ago someone like me might have enjoyed a little *nanshoku* with an eager and attractive youth, but now society and the law had changed and had affected me too. I was not tempted by Tensa, though I was very fond of him. I thought it was a boyish thing that he would grow out of and anyway, it was no barrier to marriage.

Shigure and Teru were whispering in the corner of the living room and then they both started giggling, Teru hiccuping a little through her tears. My wife and I went in to join them.

Shigure   I said we should swap husbands. Tensa would suit me perfectly. I don't want to have *marital relations*. He would leave me time to write and when he was home he would make me laugh. I like Yūdai too. Teru would be happy with Renzō – he makes lots of money and he wants to have *marital relations* all the time.

If only we could arrange life as we arrange stories. My two daughters were not really alike but there was a family resemblance. I briefly imagined a farce wherein we simply sent them back to the other's husband. Would the men even notice? How amusing it could be!

Teru   Father! You are not to write about us!
Sei   Did I say anything about making up a story?
Teru   You had that look in your eyes.
Tae   The glazed look like a dying carp?

Teru	That's the one!
Shigure	It was my idea. If anyone writes about us, it

shall be me.

Teru   At least you understand what it's like to be a woman today. Father doesn't have the first idea.

Tae   You girls don't know how lucky you are to have a father who is so indulgent. Mind you, if he hadn't spoiled you so thoroughly, we would not be in this situation now.

Once again the evening meal had fallen victim to a family crisis. I put away my plans for a bath. Tae went down the street to one of the Chinese food stalls and we all sat together in the living room and ate the dumplings she brought back. It was as though the last five years had been erased and my daughters were young girls again. Selfishly I enjoyed their company, though I was surprised at how easily they had both walked away from their husbands. Of course I blamed myself for not arranging their marriages more successfully but I wondered what was happening to women. Had they always been so wilful and demanding?

These domestic dramas had the effect of making my writing stall. The house was noisy and my anxieties ruined my concentration. I slept badly and woke very early. One morning, a few days later, it was hardly light when I opened my eyes, but I knew I would not get back to sleep. I got up, let Aka off his chain, and lit a pipe, smoking it on the side verandah while I watched him patrol our street and deposit a neat turd in the muddy depression that passed for a gutter in front of Hirano's. It was raining a little and his russet coat was beaded with moisture. He was scraping with his back legs when Yamagishi Takayuki came out of the lodging house.

Takayuki made no attempt to conceal himself, yet there was something a little secretive about the way he looked swiftly up and down the street. Aka barked at him in his gruff, non-family way, but Takayuki ignored him and walked quickly and silently away. It was like a disappearing act. One moment he was there, the next he was gone.

Aha, I thought. *I wonder who you spent the night with.*

Shigure came out carrying a cup of tea for me.

Shigure   Father, have you read my story yet?

Sei   No, I've been too busy.

Shigure   Standing on the verandah snooping?

Sei   I am not snooping! I am observing and thinking. I am studying my characters.

Shigure laughed and went back inside. I drank the tea, watched the man who worked the night shift return to Hirano's and saw one of the students leave, unshaven and still chewing on a last mouthful of breakfast. The rain cleared and the sun came out. Everything steamed.

Takayuki had been with Michi, I was sure of it.

I dressed quickly and ate a bowl of rice, leaving the rest (ignoring my wife's protests) to go outside again and wait until Michi came out. Then I walked towards her so our paths would cross, Aka trotting cheerfully along beside me. She had a piece of paper in her hand, an address, I thought.

Sei	Good morning!
Michi	Good morning, Master. You know this district

well, don't you? Where is this place? Dr Kida's clinic?

Sei	I can show you. I'm walking that way.
Michi	If it's not too much trouble.
Sei	No trouble at all.

She seemed tired and her face had that bruised look women get after making love. I fancied I could still smell the man's lingering presence on her and see the marks of his hands on her neck and throat. It was what I had predicted but I was still shocked, and shamefully envious, that she should be so bold. Ideas were racing through my mind: he had forced her, his passion had been too strong . . .

Michi   I have an introduction to Dr Kida. He's going to take me on as a student and help me prepare for the examination. Yamagishi Takayuki arranged it for me.

Her slight smile as she spoke his name was hardly that of a violated woman, and as we continued to walk towards the clinic, talking, I concluded no man would ever force Itasaki Michi into doing anything she did not want to. She would probably kill him first.

Michi   It's a very important connection. My family back in Chōshū – Yamaguchi prefecture, I should say – are depending on me getting a licence.

Sei   It must be hard for you so far from home. Do you find the work difficult?

45

Michi   The work isn't at all difficult. I know most of the practical side. I have done it for years. I come from an old medical family – my grandfather was a doctor and my mother worked with him, running the practice after his death. She's a good doctor, she makes people better and relieves their pain. But you have to have a licence to practise now, and the new theory is all so hard. Mother says she can't cope with it.

Sei   So what will she do? Will she have to give it up altogether?

Michi   I suppose she'll just do midwifery. You can do that without a licence. But we have another problem; I have to get my licence, otherwise we might lose the practice. My parents adopted me – my mother is really my aunt – but they have no papers to prove it. I have been married, you know. My husband was one of my mother's students, but he died suddenly. He had a heart problem that no one ever knew about. Now my mother's brother, who is a famous and important doctor in Nagasaki, has several sons who he wants to find places for. Of course they all have licences. It is so much easier for men. He wants to send one of his sons to Yuda, my home village, to take over our clinic.

Sei   What about your father? Is he a doctor too?

Michi   He was, but he died when I was very young. It's a terrible story. He was killed by government soldiers when he went to the aid of a protester who was about to be executed unjustly. My mother blamed the Chōshū men who are now running the government, especially Inoue Kaoru, who was a childhood neighbour and knew my father in the war. She never forgave him. When I was a child I used to imagine myself taking revenge on him. I still follow his career and make note of all his movements. He has become the Foreign Minister now. He lives quite close to here, in Tsukiji. Maybe one day our paths will cross. What method should I use, Master, seeing as I don't have a sword?

Sei   Doctors have sharp instruments, don't they? Or what about poison?

Michi   Yes, poison would be best. I know a lot about poison.

She laughed, but I felt she was not really joking. Perhaps she was confiding in me like this in order to sound out her own feelings so she could listen to them through the ears of a stranger. I knew she had been pursuing her goals with single-minded ambition, persevering despite almost universal disapproval. And now Takayuki's life had collided with hers. I had not known she was a young widow – she went by her family name of Itasaki – but it explained her audacity and lack of fear. Life was particularly difficult for women who had lost their husbands. They were supposed to be faithful to the dead and retire from the world of sex and desire, but once that desire was awakened it would always demand satisfaction. Widows were usually portrayed as comic or pathetic, dyeing their hair and pursuing younger men, but I did not think Michi fitted that mould.

We came to Dr Kida's house, in a quiet street in Shintomi 4-chome. Michi hesitated at the gate. While we were standing there two patients arrived and she moved aside so they could go in.

Michi   Do you know the doctor? What's he like?

Sei   I knew him years ago. He tried to save my son's life, but failed. I have not been here since.

Michi's gaze met mine and suddenly my eyes filled with tears. Why on earth was I weeping now when I had been dry-eyed for so long? And why had I spoken, after so many years of silence, of the four-year-old whose face I could barely recall? When he died I had felt I could not wallow in grief. I had my work to do, my family to support, my disciples to set an example for. And anyway, there was enough weeping and grieving going on with my wife and three daughters, as well as my mother, who was still alive then, their pain adding to my own.

I started doing a lot of touring at that time and while I was away it was as though I had never had a son. At home I got into the habit of leaving the room if anyone mentioned him and soon no one did anymore. And now here I was, on the verge of weeping uncontrollably in front of this young woman with her calm face and steady eyes. I turned and walked away without saying anything, came to the riverbank and crouched down with my face in my palms.

Aka sat close to me, panting in the heat.

I DID NOT WANT to talk to my wife or face sorting out our daughters' lives but it was too hot to walk around the city so, after I had composed myself, I went home.

Shigure was outside sweeping in front of the house. When the girls were little we had had a maid but once they were old enough Tae decided it would save us money if they did the housework and they would learn useful skills for married life. After they left home we never got around to finding another maid, and now they were back Tae had set them to work again.

Tae served up the remainder of my breakfast, now cold, and scolded me a little but for some reason her heart was not really in it. She sat down opposite me, her eyes on my face. I wondered what she saw there. I was relieved when Teru came in and sat down with us. She was carrying a cloth bag from which she took two balls of brightly coloured yarn and two long needles, holding a half-completed shawl.

Sei   What on earth is that?

Teru   It's knitting, Father. It's all the rage now. I taught myself from one of Mother's magazines. They sell the wool in a shop in Ginza, and they'll buy the shawls back if they are well enough made.

Sei   You are like a samurai daughter, learning to weave to support your family.

Teru   Weaving is hard work, I should think. Knitting is fun – but who said I was going to support you? Maybe I just want some money for myself so I can be an independent woman!

Sei   Can you imagine a samurai girl saying that to her family?

Teru   I'm just joking!

She showed me the process of looping the wool, stitch by stitch, until an entire garment was created. It was intriguing, and when I went to my study I saw my story in a new and pleasing way, all the different coloured threads being knitted together. I spent a long time thinking about it though I did not make much progress with the actual writing.

The day went by, punctuated by its usual rhythms. Various sellers called at the door – *Eggs! Tofu!* – and Tae had a bit of a chat with each of them. Two creditors came by, not very hopefully, I imagined: the charcoal dealer and the kimono maker. We still had not paid for Shigure's wedding kimono; I wondered if we could ask for a refund in the case of a divorce. Tae got rid of them with her usual mix of outrage and promises, but they reminded me not only of my debts to them but also of the rent I owed Hirano, which was mounting up month by month. Once I started thinking about money, any inspiration, coloured threads and all, dried up. Instead I went on to worrying about our daughters, and then I could not prevent myself from thinking about our son and the desperate heart-stopping terror that struck me when Dr Kida's face turned sombre and he shook his head.

All this depressed me. At the end of the afternoon I went to the bathhouse. It was crowded, people needing some relief from the sultry weather. The bathhouse had been closed for several weeks recently for renovations, and when it reopened it was divided into separate sections for men and women. Before, everyone had bathed together, but this was another custom that apparently offended Western sensibilities and was now frowned upon. Our local bathhouse had taken a long time to conform but eventually it had had to modernise.

I knew that the naked human body was a favourite subject in Western art and sculpture but it had never been so in Japan. Even *shunga*, the erotic prints I was so fond of, didn't usually show people without clothes – indeed the clothed bodies and the combining of different fabrics added to the eroticism. I used to enjoy going to the bathhouse and seeing male and female bodies naked in an entirely different and rather innocent way, marvelling at the many varieties of the same set of parts: head, torso, limbs, hands, feet, hair (mostly), eyes, teeth (usually), ears, genitals. Once the sexes were separated, it seemed to increase prurience rather than prevent it as it was supposed to – another puzzle of modern life!

I was thinking about this as I washed myself all over (paying particular attention to my toenails) when someone addressed me. I turned to see Yamagishi Takayuki.

A bathhouse attendant had been scrubbing his back but he made a sign for him to leave and we rinsed ourselves before getting into the hot bath side by side. Takayuki seemed to be in a talkative mood. I did not say much, firstly because close up and naked he was a powerful presence, like a warrior from the past, strong muscles, especially in his right, sword-fighting arm, flat belly and long legs. Then because, when he turned his attention on me, speaking gravely in a rather old-fashioned way and with great deference, it was impossible not to feel flattered, and finally because I could not rid myself of the image of that body on top of Michi, covering her, that voice seducing her. I felt embarrassed and ashamed. Eventually the hot water calmed me down and I could listen properly to what Takayuki was saying.

He told me what a great admirer he was of my work, how he had been wanting to get to know me better and so on and so on, until my head was swelling to the size of a melon and I found myself agreeing to accompany him to some meeting he was going to. I could quite understand how both Kyu and Michi had come under his spell. I was half in love with him myself.

We dressed and Takayuki collected a long object rolled in an old silk robe which he must have left with the bathhouse owner. I guessed immediately it was a sword. It was some years since the samurai had had to give up wearing their traditional two swords in public, laying them 'away in storehouses in tears', but I did not think there was any law against carrying a wrapped-up sword. It sat comfortably over Takayuki's right shoulder as we walked to Nihonbashi and then turned to the west, skirting the back of the Imperial Palace. It was still light, the sky a pale violet colour, the streets teeming with people making the most of the cool of the evening. Pleasure boats decorated with lanterns plied up and down the river, carrying customers to teahouses. The water lapped against the dock, ruffling the fronds of the willows. I rather wished we were going to take one of the boats and sit somewhere under the fresh green leaves where we'd eat grilled fish and have a drink or two. I was hungry after the bath and the thought came to me that this was exactly what Tae would think I was doing and she was probably grumbling about me right now.

Takayuki walked on with a swift and determined gait. People gave way to him and apologised if they brushed against him, as though they feared he might bring the sword out of hiding and cut them down.

Once past the Imperial Palace we entered the maze of side streets and alleys that had not changed since the days when the city was called Edo, and then walked uphill past a couple of former minor daimyōs' mansions, which were gradually crumbling away beneath rank grass and bamboo gone wild. No one would bother to repair them in this unfashionable district and probably someone like my son-in-law Ono Renzō would buy the land, knock the buildings down and put up cheap housing. Thinking about this reminded me of the loan I had been hoping to ask him for and now would not be able to, unless I could persuade Shigure to return to him.

Night was falling. The old grounds round the mansions were filled with dark shadows and chirping insects. Owls called from the trees. There must have been a pond nearby as frogs were croaking loudly, falling silent at the sound of our footsteps and then starting up again. It was a perfect setting for a ghost story and I could not prevent my imagination from roaming through haunted mansions, hidden documents, long-lost children, the revenge of sons and so on.

On the other side of the road was a grove of tall trees around a small shrine. Even though I had lived in Tokyo all my life, I had not walked up here before and I had not known the shrine existed. The main building was closed and dark, the usual offerings of flowers – a branch of jasmine, some marigolds – scattered on the steps along with a couple of summer oranges, but a torch lit a paved path that led behind the shrine, past a cistern, to a small hall which gleamed with light.

I followed Takayuki's example and poured water over my hands and rinsed my mouth before going towards the building.

A young man was standing at the door as if keeping guard. He bowed deeply to Takayuki and less reverently to me and, without saying anything, indicated we could enter. Slipping out of our sandals, we stepped up into the hall.

It was lit with candles and lamps but they could not dispel the darkness that hung in the rafters and the corners or give enough light to show clearly the faces of the thirty or so men who sat cross-legged on the matting. At the front of the room was a small table, like an altar, on which two black vases filled with scarlet peonies flanked an object shrouded in a gold-embroidered red silk cloth. An empty sword rack stood in front of the altar, and on the wall behind hung two portraits on either side of a banner inscribed with Chinese characters. When my eyes adjusted to the light I could see the portraits were of Saigō Takamori and Kusunoki Masashige, and the characters spelled out 'Black Ocean'.

I did not know what that meant, but naturally I was familiar with both Saigō and Kusunoki, and even had stories about them in my repertoire. They were both glorious failures of the type we Japanese love so much. Though their lives were centuries apart, both opposed the rule of the shoguns, the military dictators who in theory governed the country for the Emperor but in fact tyrannised their Imperial Majesties along with everyone else. Kusunoki was famous for his loyalty to the Emperor Go-Daigo, who had tried to challenge the shogun back in the fourteenth century, while Saigō, one of the leaders in the overthrow of the last shogun, was a hero to many samurai who felt, like him, that change had come too quickly and at too great a cost to their class. National conscription had ended their status as a warrior elite, education was giving new opportunities to commoners and women, and the despised merchants were amassing not only wealth but also political influence.

Almost the first thing Saigō had wanted to do after the Restoration was invade Korea. The Koreans had somehow ignored and insulted the new government; they needed to be taught a lesson; all other civilised nations had colonies; Japan should have some too; Korea pointed like a dagger at the heart of Japan's security and so on and so on. Saigō had the true samurai disdain for the constraints of reality and was not swayed by the fact that his government had no money and barely any armed forces. He lost the argument over Korea and resigned, retired to Satsuma, his domain, and joined the subsequent rebellion. Defeated in battle, he took his own life.

So, I thought, here we have the great Saigō and the noble Kusunoki symbolising nostalgia for the clearcut loyalties of the past. I guessed the covered portrait must be of the Emperor. While there had been efforts – photographs, public appearances, processions round the country – to make the Emperor seem more human, these were not universally popular; many still believed it was an offence to look upon the divine countenance. With these ingredients added to the stewpot, I was now getting an idea of what company I was in and what fare would be presented.

Takayuki took me to the front of the room and we bowed to the assembly, who I could now see were a mixture of tough-looking *sōshi* – not unlike Ushiwa, except of course they would hold opposing views (one of them could easily have given him the black eye at Gunma) – and men who were more elegantly dressed and of higher status. We sat down in the first row next to one of these, an older man who greeted me politely and told me his name, Terauchi Kōzō. When I began to introduce myself, he smiled slightly and said they knew very well who I was and were honoured by my presence.

Takayuki unwrapped his sword with reverent fingers and, facing the altar with bowed head, held it to his forehead and then outwards, offering it to the Emperor. He went forward on his knees, placed the sword in the rack and prostrated himself. When he moved back beside me I could see there really were tears in his eyes.

Around us rose low murmurs of approval and a few quiet *banzai*, wishes that he and the Emperor might live a thousand years, then silence fell again, a silence that seemed full of respect and devotion.

Terauchi moved to the front, sat on a cushion and began to address us. He could have been a storyteller – he even held a fan (the candles made the hall very hot), though he did not have a handtowel, which was a shame as I saw several instances where a prop would have helped him make a point; also his forehead was slick with sweat. His delivery was clear and effective; he knew how to use the dramatic pause and he was a master of quietness, dropping his voice on important sentences so everyone strained to hear.

All the same, his language was archaic and difficult, the atmosphere in the hall was stifling, the smoke was making my eyes smart, the talk seemed to go on forever and I suddenly found myself on the verge of sleep, even, I feared, emitting a tiny snore. To stay awake I stared at the sword: it seemed to be an unusually fine example, not that I knew much about swords. I made a note of every detail of its hilt and scabbard, and then I tried to make a mental list of the main points of the speech, which seemed to be:

1. Revere the Emperor and the nation.
2. Stand fast with your comrades in our secret society, Black Ocean, and preserve the traditions of the past (courage, loyalty and so on and so on).
3. Put an end to the squandering of government money on follies like the Deer Cry Pavilion.
4. Stop pandering to Western governments and demand the reform of all unequal treaties.
5. Influence or get rid of moderate ministers (bribe, cajole, intimidate and so on and so on).
6. Prepare public opinion for the invasion of Korea!

The Deer Cry Pavilion was a Western-style mansion built by Inoue Kaoru for ballroom dancing and bazaars, and the idea of these samurai indulging in a little gentle waltzing was so incongruous it made me want to laugh. Inoue was mentioned more than once; he was blamed for the troublesome problem of the treaties, and was one of the moderate ministers to be eliminated from the scene. Nobody wished him a thousand years of life.

When Terauchi spoke about Korea, Takayuki glanced at me and a few things began to edge towards each other in my mind and conglomerate there: the kabuki play about Hideyoshi's invasion, Takayuki's Korean protégé, who had been given a job in the theatre . . . so Black Ocean hoped to employ a storyteller in their campaign as well? It was not quite what I had in mind when I had begun to think Yamagishi Takayuki might make a good character in my own story.

THE TALK FINALLY came to an end and the audience began to disperse. I couldn't help noticing the unusual respect with which Terauchi and one or two others bade goodnight to Takayuki, and I began to wonder if there was something I should know about his rank. He had been extremely deferential to me, which I had, perhaps immodestly, accepted as my due. I was after all nearly twice his age and had some fame in Tokyo. But maybe I should have been deferring to him. I tried to broach the subject as we walked back down the hill. Takayuki replied that we had many things to discuss and suggested we should go to a teahouse. I was faint with hunger and I agreed. He led me to a place called Bakan, which seemed to be a haunt of rickshaw men and grooms, but behind the main area were a few small rooms right over the river. The one we went into was pleasantly cool and more elegant than I had expected. We sat down and a very jovial man immediately brought sake and a dish of paper-thin slices of raw fish. The slight prickle on my tongue told me it was *fugu* – puffer fish. Bakan was another name for Shimonoseki, the port in Yamaguchi prefecture famous for its puffer fish, so I tried to reassure myself that the cook should know how to prepare it without poisoning us. All the same, I wished I had let Takayuki try it first!

Takayuki   I like this place. The food is excellent and it's very private.

Sei   I have not been here before.

Takayuki   What did you think of the talk?

Sei   Very interesting. Mr Terauchi is certainly an accomplished speaker.

Takayuki   He is a wonderful man. I owe everything to him. His family were hereditary elders in our former domain. After my parents and brothers all died within months of each other, he took an interest in my education and wellbeing.

Sei   Yet I couldn't help noticing he treats you with some deference. Were your family high-ranking too?

Takayuki   Not particularly, lower than his. Of course there's the cherished tradition that we are descended from the Southern Emperors, but half the samurai families in Chōshū make the same claim.

Sei   I thought I might have been too familiar. If I was, please forgive me. Or if you are some long-lost prince or have performed acts of bravery I know nothing about, please enlighten me.

Takayuki   So I don't imagine it? You see it too? To be honest, I don't understand it. It bothers me. I have done nothing to deserve it. My life is ordinary: I practise in a sword-fighting school; I meditate in the Zen style; I amuse myself and earn a little money gambling at cards or on horses. Yet Lord Terauchi and the others continue to support me and protect me, as though they know something about me that I do not.

Sei Perhaps your father did them some great service and they are repaying a debt of honour. If you don't mind my asking, how did he die?

Takayuki He passed away at the end of 1866. I was only ten years old; it was in the last years of the Tokugawa rule and the country was in turmoil. My oldest brother had been killed a few months earlier fighting for Chōshū against the shogun's forces, and my mother died soon afterwards, from a broken heart, people said. Food was very scarce and we were all more or less starving. I don't remember much; I was too young and anyway grief blanks out memory. One day I got up in the morning and my father and brother were not there. I was told my father had been summoned to Kyoto; later I wondered if it was to negotiate the peace settlement between Chōshū and Tokugawa Yoshinobu, who had just become shogun. My second brother, who was now his heir, naturally went with him.

Sei They passed away in Kyoto?

Takayuki So I was told.

Sei Both of them?

Takayuki Apparently there was a smallpox epidemic. The Emperor himself perished. For years I did not believe they were dead, or if they were, I thought they might have been murdered. I used to fantasise about tracking their murderers down and taking revenge. When I was older, Lord Terauchi took me to Kyoto and showed me their graves in Ryōzen.

I can hardly remember my father now but I dream about my brother often. He is usually on horseback – he loved horses. He taught me how to ride and how to spot a good horse. It's useful at the racetrack. I sometimes wonder if he is trying to tell me something from the other world or if he is not really dead and is looking for me. What do you think, Master?

I thought both theories had great potential as plot lines, but I was not sure how to reply. More dishes arrived accompanied by another flask of sake. Takayuki studied me for a moment, then refilled my glass. For a while we ate and drank in silence. The teahouse was quiet. It was getting late; around us the city was settling down for the night like a giant animal snorting and scratching itself before sleep.

Takayuki   So you cannot solve my mystery?

Sei   I can think of many explanations but they are just a storyteller's fancies. I suppose only Mr – Lord – Terauchi can tell you the truth.

Takayuki   I have tried to ask him but he always silences me and forbids me to continue.

Sei   Then he has some secret he is hiding from you.

Takayuki   I have come to the same conclusion. But that was not my purpose in inviting you tonight.

Sei   It was not for the pleasure of my company?

Takayuki   That, of course, but it was suggested to me that since I was acquainted with you I might approach you and ask a favour. I belong to the group of patriots you met tonight – Black Ocean. We believe the time is approaching when our nation must expand. We must move into Asia and bring those backward countries into the modern era under the protection of Japan. We must start with Korea, that dagger pointing at our heart. Now, a successful invasion or annexation, whatever you call it, can only be carried out if the whole country demands it. At the moment our people don't know much about Korea. If they think about it at all it is as the exotic Hermit Kingdom, nothing to do with them. They didn't like being wakened from slumber by the Americans and their Black Ships and they don't see why we should treat Korea in the same fashion. They have been used to living in peace with their neighbours. All that has to change. They have to see that war is necessary and that Koreans need saving from themselves. If you could introduce some Korean characters into your stories, put them in a bad light, mock their backwardness – just very subtle allusions, you know the sort of thing I mean.

Sei   Eh?

Takayuki   You will be part of a trend. There will be newspaper articles, woodblock prints, the new play about Toyotomi Hideyoshi's campaigns against Korea, which I am sure your son-in-law has told you about ... but stories from someone like you, Master, would greatly help our cause. Of course, you would not go unrewarded.

Takayuki's dominating personality, along with the *fugu*, was making me very nervous and I was drinking more than I should. I found his request both offensive and intriguing, and his offer of money tempting. I wanted to please him and I wanted to write about him. I did not want to turn him away just as I was getting to know him. I did not want to antagonise Black Ocean either. But what did I know about Korea? I was searching my memory to see if I could dredge up anything, and a name drifted into my mind.

Sei   Admiral Yi!

Takayuki   Excellent! Yi's life is heroic and tragic and perfectly illustrates the cowardice and stupidity of Korean rulers. A story about him would complement the message of the play.

Sei   He should be in the play! He beat the Japanese invaders at sea – he's a hero to his people. And Hideyoshi's invasion of Korea ended in defeat. Thousands perished, Japanese and Koreans. It was a disaster – the play should be a warning not to repeat a terrible mistake.

Takayuki   Only because Hideyoshi died prematurely. Had he lived, he would have become Emperor of China.

His eyes glittered, and not only from the sake, and his right hand curled as if around a phantom sword. I could see he was reliving all the past glories of war.

Takayuki   Nothing has changed. Korea still lies under the thrall of a cruel, despotic monarch, Queen Min. And nothing will change while she is alive.

Sei   Who is Queen Min?

Takayuki gave me a brief lesson on Korean history and politics. Queen Min was the wife of the young Korean king, Gojong, and her main fault, apart from hating the Japanese with a virulent passion, seemed to be that she was an intelligent and ambitious woman who wanted to wield power herself; she had the king under her thumb (or *in her sleeve*, as Takayuki rather poetically put it) and had been locked in conflict with her father-in-law, the former regent, known as the Daewongun, until he had been whisked away by the Chinese.

By the time Takayuki had finished my head was swimming, and when I got home I was not sure if I had made any commitment or not. Tae was still up – I could not remember her ever going to bed before me – and though she grumbled at me, she was too tired and too eager to lie down to drag things out. She fell asleep quickly but I had had too much to drink; the futon moved around like a raft at sea and my mouth and tongue felt encrusted as if with barnacles. When I did sleep, I dreamed my tongue was heavy with shells. It pulled me into the ocean where I drowned, under the pitiless eyes of the Korean queen.

I HAD A TERRIBLE hangover the next day and could not face food or drink. Tae made me some barley tea and she and Teru went out to the wool shop. Teru had finished her shawl and was going to sell it. Shigure had disappeared somewhere too. I was alone in the house, sipping the tea, a damp towel on my aching head, when Aka yelped happily and someone called at the door.

It was my son-in-law Tensa. I thought I should assume a stern expression but it was not easy to maintain when at the same time I was trying to dispel nausea and hoping I was not suffering from *fugu* poisoning. Tensa put on a passable act of looking apologetic.

| Tensa | Oh! Rough night, eh? |
| Sei | Same old story, me and sake. |

Tensa   Master, I've come to apologise. You know my affection and respect for you and your family. But . . . well . . . Teru's out, isn't she?

Sei   Yes, she's gone shopping with her mother.

Tensa   I thought so. Actually I waited out of sight until I saw her leave. Does she want a divorce? I'll make no objection if she does. I'll return the wedding gifts.

Sei   I don't know. She's upset and disappointed. We haven't talked about what she wants to do next. My youngest daughter has also come home, but for different reasons. I'm half-expecting my oldest to turn up too.

Tensa   One returning daughter is a misfortune but somehow more than one is comical.

Sei   Well, don't go making up a tale about it. I don't want to become a laughing stock. There's no need for divorce, though. If I may speak frankly, you aren't the first married man to seek pleasure elsewhere with other men or women. You just have to do your duty at home and give your wife a child. One would be enough, probably. It's not too much to ask.

Tensa   I know. That's what I keep telling myself. But I can't seem to manage it. I get close to performing the act . . . and I shrink. I am terrified of the . . . you know . . . that place we are all squeezed out from, that inner depth, that cave. Well, I don't want to talk about your daughter. It's too embarrassing. It's nothing to do with her. She tries really hard. It's touching to see what efforts she makes to be a good wife. But the fact is, I have absolutely no desire to sleep with her, whereas Yūdai and I cannot keep our hands off each other. I literally cannot spend a day without him. That sort of bond is rare. I did not ask to feel it for another man, but there you are – I do feel it.

He is my lover, my companion, my colleague, and I hope he will be forever.

To me it did not seem so very different from the idealised romantic bonds between warrior comrades in Bakin and other past writers.

Sei   It may not actually be illegal but these days it is certainly not approved of. If you get a divorce and continue living with Yūdai, everyone will suspect why. There will be gossip – it could affect your career.

Tensa   I can't expect Teru to stay with me just to give me a cover.

Sei   I don't suppose she would be willing to do that anyway. I am sure she wants to have children.

A mournful expression came over Tensa's face and we sat in silence for a few minutes.

Tensa   So what were you up to last night, Master? Don't tell me you've been playing away from home too!

Sei   You won't believe me, but the urge wears off when you get to my age. I went to a meeting and then I drank too much afterwards with the man who took me there. And I ate *fugu* – I'm afraid it didn't agree with me.

Tensa   A political meeting?

Sei   I suppose so.

Tensa   You must have been feeling reckless! *Fugu* and politics in the same evening!

Sei   It was an organisation called Black Ocean, a secret society. I'd never heard of them.

Tensa   Can't say I have either. But then they wouldn't be very secret if we had!

Sei   They had a strange request. Tell me, would you put particular characters in a story you were telling, to influence the way people think about other nations?

Tensa   You mean foreign characters? Well, they're often good for a laugh: the Englishman with his roast beef and his milky smell, the French ladies who ogle rickshaw drivers while pretending to be shocked at their undress, the tall Germans with large bosoms dancing in the arms of men half their size.

Still kneeling, Tensa took out his fan and demonstrated, making me smile despite my headache and inclining me to forgive him everything simply because he was so talented.

Tensa   Foreigners are pretty funny when you come to think of it – their speech, clothes, looks, habits.

Sei   What about Koreans?

Tensa   I don't know that I've ever told a comic tale about Koreans. They're not a great source of jokes. I suppose there's the language – it sounds like Japanese but you can't understand a word. And kimchi, a splendid dish of pure fieriness; heavy metal chopsticks which are more like weapons; dog stew, so your fat Aka would have to watch out. And doesn't the Hill of Ears have something to do with Koreans? I saw it last time I was in Kyoto. I've always thought there might be a story behind that, but it's probably not a comedy. They have tigers on the streets of Seoul, I believe. They call out in the voice of a woman to entice men to them so they can devour them.

Sei   So that's why you're afraid of women?

Tensa   Yes, they're all tigers in disguise. This organisation, Black Ocean, sounds rather shady – why do they want you to tell stories about Koreans? I presume to disparage them? Quite a droll idea, isn't it? I wonder who they are exactly?

Sei   They seem to have some important connections.

Tensa   If I can give you some advice, Master, if you don't despise me completely, you should avoid getting involved with them. Apart from any other danger, the moment you start writing to someone else's instructions your story will die on you.

Aka yelped outside and Tensa jumped up. He shot out of the front door just as his wife and mother-in-law came in through the side.

I WOULD HAVE LIKED to go back to bed but the usual morning clamour and clatter was arising all around and my head was aching too much to sleep. Shigure appeared at my side and fixed me with a questioning stare. I still had not read her story but I said hurriedly I had some chores to attend to and got ready to go out. I thought I might go to the local barber and have a shave and a haircut.

As I walked past Hirano's, Chie, who was outside watering the pots of flowers she kept around the entrance, called out to me.

Chie   Good morning, Master. Thanks for the rent money. We weren't expecting you to pay it in full.
Sei   Eh?
Chie   A messenger brought it round first thing this

morning. We're really very grateful. Come by later and see my husband – he's not up yet.

Sei   Beautiful flowers. They really are very . . . beautiful.

Chie   You should have brought it yourself. No need to be so formal. Or maybe someone else paid it for you?

She had worked in some minor geisha house before she married. She knew all about buying and selling.

Sei   Yes, it's an interesting story – a long-lost friend, a great admirer, became a very rich man, sadly died just after we were reunited, left me a large sum of money. I instructed the lawyers . . .

And with this flagrant lie I walked on, possessed in equal amounts by surprise, relief and apprehension.

While I was under the soothing hands of the barber, in the steamy atmosphere of his shop, my mind became slightly unhinged and all sorts of dramatic possibilites began to suggest themselves. Queens, admirals, invaders, love triangles, jealousy, poisons, swords, intrigue, intimidation, blackmail: the razor at my throat hinted at murder, the whispered conversations around me at assignations and conspiracies. I remembered that the loss of self-control allows both demons and angels to emerge. I could sense their imminent arrival. I just had to prepare myself to welcome them.

In this state, my body suffering but clean shaven, my mind racing, I decided to walk over to Kanda and visit the bookshops, just to inform myself a little better about Korea before I made any decisions. Maybe an irresistible story would jump out at me like a tiger in the streets of Seoul.

I wandered down the crowded street among the book lovers, picking up a book here and there, skimming, putting it down again. I was used to reading this way; it was one of my small economies. I had promised myself I would buy no more books until I had read all the ones I already possessed at home.

There were several so-called 'true histories' of the Bunroku and Keichō invasions of Korea (named for the years in which they took place, 1592 and 1598), but they were mostly concerned with the heroic exploits of the Japanese – the swift marches, bloody but victorious battles, stubborn sieges and so on and so on. Unfortunately for Takayuki, even in these biased records, the best stories were about Koreans – like the young woman who, closely embracing her samurai 'lover' (rapist, more likely), leaped over a cliff with him to their death on the rocks below. And of course, Admiral Yi, to whom an entire linked story lasting days and days would hardly do justice.

Around midday I ventured to eat a bowl of hot noodles, thinking it might settle my stomach a little, and I took a moment to reflect on my circumstances. I was annoyed that Takayuki (it could only be him) should think I was so easily manipulated. I felt like an object in a pawnshop. He had paid my debts in such a way that it was going to be hard to redeem myself. I could not very well demand the money back from the Hiranos, especially after lying to Chie. On the other hand, it was a great relief to have the burden of my rent removed. I wondered if it might not be so very hard to meet Takayuki's demands. Surely I could find a story to tell about Korea.

The noodles had the opposite effect from the one I had hoped for and my bowels were churning. I needed the privy urgently. There was a shop over the road whose owner, Kuruba Gozaemon, I knew quite well, and I hurried across as fast as I could through the congested mass of rickshaws and people going nowhere in particular yet complaining how long it took them. Gozaemon kindly showed me out the back and I got there just in time.

When I returned to the shop his assistant brought us some tea and I told Gozaemon about my new-found interest in Korea.

Gozaemon   Korea, Korea! Suddenly Korea is popular. You're the fourth person I've had in this week asking for books or prints on Korea, Katō Kiyomasa, Konishi Yukinaga and so on. Why do these fashions occur?

Sei   Mysterious, isn't it? It happens with storytelling. All at once we all come up with a new story on the same theme. It's like an infection.

Gozaemon   You make it sound unpleasant, like measles or cholera. Speaking of stories, I heard the Englishman last night, Jack Green. What a performance! You should try to catch it, Master. He told an English tale about an orphan. His stories are so exotic and he has a thrilling delivery.

Sei   Yes, I've heard him. He really is very good. So do you have anything left on Korea?

Gozaemon   To read or to buy?

Sei   That depends, I suppose.

Gozaemon   I've got something rather unusual. I haven't shown it to anyone else. I bought a load of manuscripts from a temple – the collection of an eighteenth-century abbot. The temple's being relocated to make way for a railway station and when they discovered these weren't exactly sacred texts they decided to sell them. The old abbot must have been quite racy – there's a lot of *nanshoku* tales and *shunga*. And then there was this diary of a monk who accompanied one of the commanders in the sixteenth-century invasions of Korea. It's not the original – I haven't been able to discover where that is, but it's quite an old copy. I can let you have a look at it, but I must warn you, Master, I'm asking fifty yen for it and that's a special price for you.

Fifty yen was two months' salary for most public servants, quite a staggering sum for a book. Of course I didn't have it. But it was also about the same amount Takayuki had paid Hirano for my overdue rent, so on the other hand I was no longer *minus* fifty yen. Gozaemon smirked a bit at my expression, ushered me into the back room, took out the volume, wrapped in an old cloth, and gave it to me.

A customer called out from the front and he left me alone to read.

This was a very different account from the glorious histories I had been reading so far. The monk, Keinen, wrote with horror and compassion of the 'Buddha-less hell' of the second invasion: starving people, civilians and soldiers who ate not only dogs but cats, rats, leather, leaves, mud from walls and finally each other; the stench of putrefying flesh; soldiers insane with blood lust decapitating everything living, even animals; men tortured and beaten to death, noses cut off for grisly body counts. It was too nauseating for me to read much but I was transfixed. I had to buy it.

While I was waiting for Gozaemon to return I was suddenly overcome by exhaustion. My eyes closed and I fell into a kind of doze, my hands still holding the diary. The doze turned into a short, intense dream. I couldn't remember it when I woke up but I had a sense of a presence beside me, so strong I turned to see if someone had sat down next to me and was reading over my shoulder. There was no one there but I thought I smelled a slight whiff of decay.

I might have mentioned that I have a very sensitive sense of smell and sometimes I smell things that are not really there. I read a passage in a book or listen to a description and immediately smell incense or seaweed, the sweat of horses, the scent of jasmine. So I thought it was no more than a hallucination brought on by Keinen's vivid descriptions and probably made worse by alcoholic or *fugu* poisoning.

Gozaemon came back, rubbing his hands. We haggled a bit over the price. I knew there were not many people he could sell this book to; he knew I was desperate to have it. In the end we agreed on forty yen, which made me feel I was still in credit in the skewed balance book of my mind. I paid him all the money I had on me as a deposit and signed a note for the rest. As I left he suggested quietly that I might like to keep the book hidden. There had to be a reason it had never been published and the picture it drew was not that of the civilised nation we were trying to become.

I WENT OUTSIDE INTO what passed for fresh air on a hot Tokyo afternoon. Any lingering smell was masked by the stenches of the city. Yet I still had the sense that I was accompanied by someone, walking just behind my right shoulder, keeping step with me. I had said I would be prepared for angels or demons to visit me, but I had not meant it literally. I had a headache and the dark patches around the edges of my vision were made worse by the glare. Maybe that was the cause of the semi-hallucination. But that made me think of going blind. I thought I would rather be possessed by any supernatural being than lose my sight.

On the corner of my street I came across Okuda Satoshi, Hirano's lodger who had been in France, talking to Michi. Her clothes were bloodstained and her face pale as if from shock. It was a sign of how much I was still caught up in Keinen's world that I was not overly surprised by this, almost as though the blood had seeped from the pages of his narrative.

Satoshi   I thought Miss Itasaki had hurt herself . . . I stopped to inquire.

Michi   I have been operating at the clinic. I killed someone today – this is the blood of one of my patients.

Satoshi   It must happen inevitably in your profession. You must have seen many people die.

Michi   Operations are always dangerous – the anaesthetics, shock, loss of blood, sepsis. Dr Kida was testing me. I had to remove a tumour but it was not possible to do it without severing major blood vessels. I got the tumour out but the patient died.

Satoshi   Was that considered a success or a failure?

Michi   Success for me; I operated well and my teacher was quite pleased.

Satoshi   Not so successful for your patient.

Michi   I wish I could have saved him, but he was going to die anyway. So Dr Kida told me afterwards. Well, I must go and wash, and then – back to the books!

Satoshi and I watched her walk to the lodging house, probably with identical expressions on our faces. Her masculine assurance, her feminine appearance, the way she spoke of killing in her soft voice were overwhelmingly attractive. Of course I was beyond all that at my age; I just wanted to capture her unusual character for my story, but Satoshi, I could see, was completely smitten. Poor fellow, he could not know about Takayuki!

Satoshi   Such an admirable woman! Her story is heroic in its own way. If I could write I would write a novel about her in the French style. Or poems. If only I were a Baudelaire!

He murmured something poetic in a foreign language which I assumed was French.

Satoshi   If you have time, Master, come inside. I'll show you my books and we can talk about plots and the way they write about love in France.

Sei   I would like that, though I must not stay long. And I must warn you, I have given up alcohol.

Satoshi   I can't afford to buy sake anyway, so I won't tempt you. I indulged rather too much myself last night with Mr Hirano. I didn't even know he existed before that. Does he never move from that room?

Sei   It's years since I've seen him outside.

Satoshi   He serves a very fine sake and he knows a surprising amount about French political history. I met an activist there too, a man called Ushiwa. You probably know him.

Sei   Yes, I know Ushiwa.

Satoshi   He's invited me to speak at one of his meetings, about France and the Revolution, Napoleon and so on.

Sei   I'll come and listen. Sounds interesting.

Satoshi   Would you? I'd be honoured. I was thinking, I might ask our doctor friend. Do you think she would come?

By this time we were at the door. Chie was ostensibly tidying up the entrance hall, straightening out the rows of shoes and sandals.

Chie   Oh, there you are, Master. Your wife was wondering where you'd got to. Imagine, I went over to congratulate her on your good fortune and I don't think she knew what I was talking about. You're a deep one!

I nodded and smiled in what I hoped was an enigmatic way and began to think quite without meaning to of the threads of gossip that held our neighbourhood together. When our children were infants and Tae was nursing them, she was part of a milk network – women helped each other bring down the milk for the babies and took care of the motherless ones. They knew all the special foods and herbs that boosted the milk supply and they knew all each other's secrets. Now they exchanged gossip like milk. Gossips, informants, the city was full of both, half-truths spreading from tongue to ear, tongue to ear, words changing, like in the children's whispering game. It made it very hard to keep secrets. Chie, being childless, had never been part of this circle and my wife had never confided in her. She would be furious if she thought Chie knew something about us that I had omitted to tell her. I was not looking forward to going home.

Satoshi's room was one of the smaller ones in an annexe constructed at the back of the main house, next to the night worker who had just got up and was smoking a pipe and blinking in a dazed and regretful way at the rays of the setting sun. Satoshi slid open the door and ushered me in, waving a hand grandly around the room.

Satoshi   My worldly possessions! Please sit down.

The room was furnished mostly with books, arranged in neat piles around the walls. There were both Japanese and French titles, the Japanese ones on education, literature and translation, the French ones – well, I had no idea, but Satoshi was keen to tell me. He took out a large volume (Victor Hugo, one of the names he had mentioned to me previously) and launched into the plot, a long and confused tale about an escaped criminal, stolen candlesticks, a kindly priest, shady innkeepers, an orphan girl. The story obviously had some interesting elements but Satoshi was a terrible storyteller. He kept remembering things he had forgotten to put in, went forwards and backwards, and gave away the ending. I became more and more bemused and in the end he noticed, put away that book and took out another, by a different author, one Dumas. This story was less complicated: a man, unjustly imprisoned in an impregnable castle, escapes, comes into a great deal of money, impersonates a nobleman and takes revenge on his enemies. It was a good story; revenge was always popular and I thought I might be able to use it.

Satoshi had just started talking about novels concerned with women and love when we heard steps outside and Michi came in with a tray.

Michi   Mrs Hirano asked me to bring you some tea.
Satoshi   She should not have interrupted your studies! But come and sit down with us.

Michi set down the tray and knelt on the mat to pour the tea. She had bathed and changed out of her work clothes into a light cotton yukata patterned with scarlet goldfish. She smelled damp and fragrant, the enticing smell of a young woman. I am probably protesting too much, but really I was not interested in her in that way, though poor Satoshi was.

She took up one of the books from the floor and tried to spell out the title.

Michi   I know a little English, enough to read the alphabet. What does this say?

Satoshi   *Les Fleurs du Mal:* The Flowers of Evil.

Michi   I like that.

Satoshi   By Charles Baudelaire – I'll read you my favourite poem.

He read a few verses; they had a gentle rhythm and definite rhymes; his delivery was emotional.

Michi   What does it mean?

Satoshi   'My child, my sister, imagine the joy, if we went to live up there together, and loved each other and died up there, in the country so like you. Its diffused sunshine, its misty skies, have for me the same mysterious charm as your traitor eyes, shining through tears.'

Well! I had never thought Satoshi would be so bold. I had never heard such a declaration of love. Michi was gazing at him as if the words had bewitched her. They both began to blush furiously.

Sei   Er, you must have been in France for a long time to collect so many books.

Satoshi   Yes, yes, about six years. Or was it seven? Maybe seven. My family are in the silk business in Chichibu. We dealt with many French people from Lyon. One of them invited me to spend some time there, seeing the other side of the business. But shortly after I arrived, the market collapsed and my patron went bankrupt. I could no longer remain in Lyon but I didn't want to return home without seeing Paris. I went for a week and stayed seven years.

Michi   Why does she have traitor eyes?

Satoshi   I suppose she has been involved with another man.

Michi   It made me think of somewhere in the north: Hokkaido or the Russian islands. Not that I've ever been there but it's how I imagine it.

Satoshi   I think it's about wanting to go north.

They both fell silent while I fancied the room pulsated with longing.

Sei   So what are your plans now?

Satoshi   I suppose I'll stay in Tokyo. I was offered a job in the language academy. I'll go back and see my parents but I don't want to return home to live or to work in the silk business. Maybe I'll get married.

He could not stay off the subject! I was feeling quite super-fluous. I thanked him for the story ideas and reminded him to tell me the time and place of the meeting where he was to give his lecture on France. He immediately invited Michi too. She nodded and said to me that we would go together. She left with me and walked languidly along the verandah, her face pensive.

A T HOME TAE immediately started on the money we had apparently been left by a friend she had never heard of.

Sei I did say he was long-lost!

Tae Why didn't you tell me? Is there anything left over? You didn't have to blow it all on the rent. Chie would never have been able to ask for it – we're related. We're going to need some cash with two divorces coming up and then either more weddings or two more mouths to feed at home.

Sei Look, there is no friend, long-lost or otherwise. I just told Chie that on the spur of the moment. It was the best I could come up with. Someone paid the rent, I'm not sure who.

Tae What have you got yourself into?

Sei Maybe it was a fan.

Tae　　　It's been a long time since you've had fans. Oh, I'm not saying people don't respect you for the past – you were great once. But you don't have fans now in the way the great actors do, or Jack Green.

She did not say it unkindly but her words stung more than I would have thought possible. It had been a long and tiring day. I told her I did not feel well and would lie down; I didn't want anything to eat. While she was laying out the bedding I took Keinen's diary and hid it among my other books.

I was unwell for a few days and did not go out. I wanted to start writing and yet I did not have the strength. My head was full of ideas and characters who spoke in sudden flurries and whispers yet I did not feel able to pursue them and pin them down. I spent the time reading Shigure's story.

It was in that time-honoured form, the diary, written with almost Heian-like sensitivity and delicacy. Yet the diarist was a very modern young woman, dealing with all the demands and changes of contemporary life. Her voice leaped off the page and forced you to read on. The story was simple and romantic: she falls in love with one young man, and he with her, but her old-fashioned parents want her to marry another. She obeys them dutifully. Her husband comes to adore her, but she yearns after her first love. They meet again by chance, his feelings are unchanged, he has suffered greatly from losing her. He begs her to run away with him. She goes to meet him in a thunderstorm and tells him he must forget her. They say goodbye for ever. She catches cold, which turns to pneumonia. She resigns herself to death and being with her lover in another life. Her husband's grief is pitiful, and the last diary entry on her deathbed reveals she has realised it is him she loves after all, truly and deeply.

Trite though the story was, I found myself moved by it. I forgot it was written by my daughter. Though I recognised elements of Tae and myself in the parents, they were not simply a portrait of us but fully formed characters in their own right. The writing was lively and accomplished, laced with allusions, and Shigure had captured perfectly the changing city and the hopes and fears of its inhabitants. I had to admit it was not something I could have written. I was even a little bit jealous.

I did not praise Shigure too much, nor did I tell her I was going to show her story to a friend who wrote for one of the daily newspapers. I did not want to raise her hopes unduly. But when I felt better I walked down to the newspaper office, saw my friend and asked if he would be able to give me an opinion. I did not tell him the author was my daughter.

As I was leaving I ran into my son-in-law Kat'chan, the stage manager.

Kat'chan   Master! What a fortunate coincidence. It must be fate that has brought us together. I'm looking for someone to write an article – and here you are! I thought I'd inquire at the newspaper but I would much rather keep it in the family. I don't want to be presumptuous, but there would be quite a good fee.

We went off to a teahouse to discuss it.

Kat'chan   I want you to write about the Korean. It's the most extraordinary thing – he's become extremely popular. He's only an assistant in black, but when he's on stage he's the only thing anyone looks at. He kneels, they gasp; he hands Sakutarō a sword, they all sigh. When he leaves the stage the play dies. Fans are starting to wait outside for him and yesterday pictures of him appeared on sale.

Sei   What do the actors think about that?

Kat'chan   Sakutarō is rather amused; Kyu's glory is his glory. Kenjirō is furiously jealous. The rest of the cast are bewildered, even shocked. Something like this has never really happened before. They ask themselves why it shouldn't be them and they're fed up because the owner wants to extend the season for another two weeks while audiences keep coming back. We should be starting the summer break now, you know. The other stagehands keep playing tricks on Kyu to get back at him. Yesterday someone put a cabbage where a severed head was meant to be. I should be keeping an eye on them all the time – heaven knows what they're getting up to today. But I've been told to drum up some extra publicity for the next play. So how about it? A short piece on the new kabuki phenomenon?

Sei   Is he going to be Korean or Japanese in the article?

Kat'chan   I don't know. What do you think?

Sei   Well, if he's Japanese I can just make up a life story for him but if he's Korean I need to talk to him.

Kat'chan   Maybe you should talk to him anyway and then you can decide.

We arranged that I would come to the theatre after the play the following evening. As we parted Kat'chan remarked that he would be going away to the mountains as soon as the play was over and Yuri and the boys wanted to come and stay with us.

I went home to break the news to Tae.

My manager, Rinjirō, was there, drinking tea and chatting with my wife. They were looking very friendly, rekindling my suspicions. I thought of Shigure's story. Had Tae and I ever loved each other truly and deeply? Such questions had hardly occurred to our generation. There had been times when we trembled for each other, had been joined in ecstasy and had held each other after with exquisite tenderness. Since our son's death we had grown slowly apart, unable to speak of him or to comfort each other. And that had been my fault. If my wife were having an affair with my manager I had no one to blame but myself. That didn't prevent me feeling wounded and jealous.

Rinjirō told me he had booked a large *yose* hall for me through the autumn until the end of the year. I immediately felt sick.

Rinjirō   People are very excited. I'm getting a good response; we must build on that. I'll take out advertisements in the newspapers and write some articles about you. But I need to have some idea what your new story is about.

Sei   It's too early to say yet. You know I don't like talking about stories before they're ready. It kills them.

Poor stories, such fragile, demanding creatures! So many things took the life out of them: early exposure, writing to order, resorting to stereotypes. And in my case, sheer lack of inspiration, a well run dry.

Tae   The deadline will help you get started. Nothing like a bit of pressure!

I spent the following day recording these conversations in my journal, and thinking about Kyu and what I wanted to ask him. I was not used to interviewing people – I preferred to hang around on the margins, snooping, as my daughter Shigure would say. Asking people direct questions about their lives seemed quite discourteous, and anyway, what was the point? People said whatever made them sound good or told you what they thought you wanted to hear. All through their lives, people spun stories to themselves and others that had nothing to do with reality. And, I reflected, nations naturally did the same, choosing history that glorified them and suppressing the rest.

Even diaries, which were supposed to strive after a truthful account, emphasised some things and omitted others. The journal I was writing was just a construction: a few years of my life according to me, and who would ever read it? Keinen's diary, which lay smouldering among my books like the embers of a fire, had only been read by a handful of people in three hundred years. Shigure's fictional diary might be read by thousands if it was published in a newspaper or magazine; would people discern if it were true or not?

And the story I was trying to make up? I was basing it on real people but what hope did I have of ever really knowing them? I would invent their lives and my inventions would become as real as their true ones, but in essence I would be telling lies about them, just as Takayuki expected me to tell lies about Koreans, to participate in his refurbishing of history. And what did it matter if I added my voice to the cacophony around me? How many people would hear my version? A handful of loyal old fans who were probably going deaf anyway. And now I was expected to produce a puff piece about this young man who might be Japanese or Korean – it was not yet decided.

In the evening I went down to the Shintomi-za.

It was after sunset and a full moon was rising. There was a small group of fans waiting outside. Some were carrying the prints of Kyu that Kat'chan had mentioned, depicting him in black, his face white, his lips startlingly red. It was indeed a strange phenomenon, but there was no predicting what might suddenly become the rage. Fads came from nowhere and swept through the city all the time.

Kat'chan joined me and we scooped Kyu away from his admirers and took him to a nearby teahouse. Kat'chan had arranged for us to have one of the private rooms they kept for assignations; he showed us where it was and left us there.

Kyu gazed at me with his heavy lidded eyes and remarked that this was where Sakutarō brought him; immediately I imagined I could smell semen, like almonds, the actor's perfume and his sweat. Kyu smiled slightly, as though he was aware of the eroticism that hung around the room, and my discomfort.

The maid brought tea and Kyu ordered a dish of chicken and rice, explaining he had not eaten all day. I made a few comments about the play. Then we sat in silence while he ate, hungrily and intently like a cat.

When he had finished Kyu put the tray to one side and leaned towards me.

Kyu   Do you want to . . . ?

Sei   No, no! That's not why we are here.

Kyu   I know, you want to talk to me. But I don't mind if you want to do something else beforehand. When I first got together with Sakutarō, he told me he always had to have sex after a performance, he was in such a state of arousal. Now I know how he feels.

Sei   Let's just talk. Tell me a bit about yourself.

Kyu   What sort of things do you want to know? Most of my life isn't fit to be read about in a newspaper.

His Japanese was perfect with no trace of an accent, his language the actors' mix of elegance and slang.

Sei   How did you come to work in the theatre?

Kyu   I saw the actors when I first came to Japan. I wanted to be one of them. Everyone told me it was impossible, that you had to belong to one of the traditional families, but I thought if I could only get into the theatre someone would notice me. And it worked. Now Kigawa Sakutarō is my patron; he might even adopt me and then I will be able to act.

Sei   Who got you the job backstage?

Kyu   That was Yamagishi Takayuki. It was a gift to reward me for the work I do for him. He knows how much I love the theatre.

Sei   And how did you meet Takayuki?

Kyu   He came with some thugs to beat up Mr Maeda, the man who brought me to Japan.

Sei   Not exactly an auspicious first meeting, then!

Maeda, I learned, was a Japanese merchant who traded between the ports of Yokohama and Inchon in Korea. He had picked Kyu up in Seoul and had obviously become infatuated with him. The boy was the son by a concubine of a minor Korean official who had sympathised with the Progressive Party and ended up in prison, where he died of ill-treatment and hunger. Kyu and his mother were turned out by his legal heirs. Kyu had been well educated and played several musical instruments. He eventually joined a group of musicians, and began going with men – I guessed for the affection as much as for the money.

The 'very sweet' Maeda was kind to Kyu but he was addicted to gambling and ran up huge debts with the tattooed men. The beating was the last in a string of increasingly violent incidents intended to persuade the merchant to pay his debts.

Kyu   I kicked them and cursed them. Takayuki realised I was Korean. He came back and said he could use someone who spoke both Korean and Japanese, and he would take me away somewhere safe. I was afraid they would kill Maeda next time so I went with him. He's taught me everything. I owe so much to him.

Sei   Yet you call yourself Maeda.

Kyu   My real name is Shin Kyu-hyuk but I had to have a Japanese name – Maeda was almost the only one I knew. I think I might change it.

Sei   You'd better decide quickly before you get too famous.

Kyu   It will be Kigawa, when I am adopted into that family.

Sei   Should I write about you as Japanese or Korean?

Kyu   It's become dangerous to be known as Korean

in Tokyo – just in the last few months there have been several attacks on Korean restaurants and individuals. And the Queen – you know who I mean? Queen Min? – may have spies here. I don't want to come to her attention. I would be immediately suspect because of my father's connections with Kim Ok-gyun.

Sei   I don't know who that is.

Kyu   One of the leaders of the Progressive Party. He believes Japan should help Korea modernise; he wants the Japanese to help him overthrow the government.

Sei   You're well informed.

Kyu   Takayuki often meets with Korean patriots. I translate for him. It's a strange game. It would be amusing if it were not so dangerous. Both sides use each other to advance their own cause. Kim Ok-gyun and the other patriots think they can get Japanese support without making any commitments to them. Takayuki genuinely admires Kim, I believe, but he and his associates also think they can use him to get a toehold in Korea. The only thing they agree on is that they hate the Queen. You'd better not write about that; the meetings are always kept very secret. But apart from that, I'm not stupid; I can read and write, Japanese and Korean. I keep my ears open.

Sei   So I'll call you Maeda Kyuichi?

Kyu   Just call me Kyu, everyone does.

Sei   What was it like, working under the stage?

Kyu   I loved it. It's a different world down there, frantic and dangerous, but you are making the play come to life. I fainted, though. I told Sakutarō I was overcome by my feelings for him, but that wasn't really true. I'd been sick.

Sei   Yes, I saw how Takayuki saved you from being carted off to the isolation hospital.

Kyu   He saved me and I lost him.

Sei   Eh?

Kyu   That was when he saw the doctor woman, Michi.

Sei   I remember.

Kyu   Now he is obsessed by her. He always seemed to despise women and had nothing but scorn for men who fell in love. You must know the type – his companions are all the same. Very attractive, they are so hard and manly. They model themselves on samurai of old. And now he is infatuated with this woman. I hate her!

Sei   She probably saved your life.

Kyu   I just had food poisoning. I know, she sat with me all night, washed me and held my head while I vomited, and talked to me and told me her life history. I was grateful to her; I called her my older sister. But then she stole Takayuki from me. I'll never forgive her.

I could not very well write about this in a newspaper article but it was great material for my own work. I wanted very much to ask Kyu what Michi had confided in him but could not see how to frame the question in the context of the interview I was conducting. Luckily Kyu was eager to reveal Michi's secrets.

Kyu   She confided in me that since her husband died she had lost all sense of fear. That was how she was able to live alone and study like a man. I told Takayuki this, and he decided to test her. He went to confront her with the threat of rape or maybe he intended to kill her. It was as though a woman who was not afraid was an affront to him. But whatever happened, it was not rape, and it led to his obsession.

Sei   You should not have repeated what she said.

Kyu   I can't help myself. I tell him everything. Have you never loved someone like that, when you belong to them, body and soul? I hope he is just pretending to love her in order to use her. He arranged for her to work at Dr Kida's clinic and study with him. He never does something for nothing.

Sei   What would he use her for?

Kyu   I don't know – you're the storyteller. What do you think?

Sei   I can imagine falling in love with her with no ulterior motive.

Kyu   But you are not Yamagishi Takayuki. She will spy for him; maybe she will even kill for him. Doctors have access to all sorts of poisons. And you know how she looks, innocent and serious and beautiful. She could go many places without arousing suspicion. Men are fools where a pretty woman is concerned.

Sei   Let's talk about the new play.

Kyu   It's just another rewriting of an old disaster. They should go to Seoul and listen to some of the stories of what really happened. Or ask me – but of course no one does. Still, it's got a few good scenes in it. Sakutarō's role is wonderful. And I might get to play the tiger.

Sei   Eh?

Kyu   When he wasn't slaughtering Koreans, one of Hideyoshi's commanders, Katō Kiyomasa, went tiger hunting. He sent the meat back to Hideyoshi to cure his ailing health. Kenjirō, who plays Katō, was desperate to kill a tiger on stage. I was hoping I might play the horse – Hideyoshi gives a beautiful horse to Sakutarō's character, Konishi Yukinaga – but there's a traditional kabuki dynasty who always and only play the horses; they've done it for generations and it's become just an imitation, the movements are banal and stultified, and so boring. The horse on stage should be more than real, a sort of essence of Horse. I've watched horses; I go to the racetrack with Takayuki. I showed them how horses really move and got thumped for my pains. Sakutarō was furious, and demanded if they had the tiger on stage then I should play it. I'm probably the only person in the company who's ever seen a tiger.

Sei   You have seen a tiger?

Kyu   Yes, in the forest outside Seoul. I had gone to a temple to play at a festival and a boy and I . . . noticed each other and slipped away together. We had just finished and were lying in each other's arms when I heard a twig break and saw a tiger pass not ten feet away from us. Neither of us dared move, but in fact I would not have minded dying then. The tiger was so beautiful, so alive, so completely possessed of its animal self. Ever since I saw it, I have longed to create it in some way. You must understand this – you are a sort of artist too. We all yearn to capture the world around us. Some people hunt tigers, some tame horses, some pursue characters as you do.

Sei   When you were sick, you were rambling about horses and tigers. I wondered why.

Kyu   I dreamed a lot about them at that time. I was a bit obsessed with becoming one or the other on stage, allowing that essence to possess me, representing the real through the unreal. It's more than clever artifice – I am still wrestling with it, to be honest. You will see, if I succeed, if they let me be the tiger. Kenjirō will try to prevent it. I am more popular than he is now. It infuriates him. I think I will get my way, though. I just hope someone doesn't sharpen his spear so he kills me on stage for real!

Sei　　　　How do you explain your popularity and your success on stage? Why do people look at you, a stagehand in black, rather than at the actors?

Kyu　　　　Why do you think?

He turned his full charm on me. His expressive face was infused with sexuality and life. How attractive he was! And he had offered himself to me. I was almost sorry I had refused.

Kyu　　　　That. And I am different and I am real.

I WENT HOME AND made some notes. I'd decided I would write two versions for Kat'chan, one in which Kyu being Korean was the hook on which the story hung, the other more about the new play, the horse and the tiger and a young Japanese actor's popularity. Neither would be completely false and at least some of Kyu's actual words would appear in both of them. I also wrote down all that Kyu had told me about Michi and Takayuki, fascinated by what he had revealed of their characters, and by his own unexpected depths of sensitivity and artistic feeling. I wondered how I would answer his question: I was not sure that I had ever loved anyone so profoundly or belonged to her body and soul. Only my characters and my stories obsessed me to that extent.

By the time I got ready for bed it was quite late. Tae helped me with my clothes as she always did but she seemed preoccupied and said very little. I assumed she was tired and felt a flicker of guilt at keeping her up. When we were both lying down and the light was extinguished, she spoke suddenly in a serious voice.

Tae	I've something I want to tell you.
Sei	Is it about Rinjirō?
Tae	Rinjirō? No, why should I want to talk about Rinjirō?
Sei	He's always coming round here . . . I thought . . . you might be having an affair with him.
Tae	What are you talking about? He comes round here because he's your manager.
Sei	You always seem to have a lot to say to each other, the two of you.
Tae	We're making small talk waiting for you to come home! You're out all the time till all hours – maybe you're the one having an affair!
Sei	Well, I'm not!
Tae	Neither am I, though now you've put the idea into my head . . . What I wanted to say was, I know you haven't seen Yuri's boys for a while. Sojirō, the younger one, is four now, nearly five. I wanted to warn you . . . he looks just like our Tatsuo. It would be a shock if you weren't expecting it. I didn't know how you would react. They are coming the week after next, you know, while Kat'chan goes to Mount Yari.
Sei	We will be a full house.
Tae	We won't interrupt your precious work!

I was grateful to her and moved by what she said. I felt I should hold her and say something comforting but she turned away from me, complaining about the heat. I supposed I had upset her in some way, though I had not meant to.

Just as I was about to fall asleep she spoke in the husky voice of someone who had been weeping silently.

Tae   It is fourteen years this week.

That left me wide awake, thinking about death and what happens afterwards. I had not seen much of my grandsons because they awakened such painful memories of my own son and I was so afraid for them I could not bear my anxiety. I had always wanted to distance myself from that messy, unpredictable, frightening world of birth and child-raising. There were epidemics, accidents and sudden inexplicable deaths. Women died, children died, and no one ever got used to grief. No wonder men hardened themselves and retreated into their own worlds. If we allowed ourselves to feel the anxiety and sorrow women lived with, no empires or armies would ever be created, no temples or factories built, no pictures painted or plays written. We left home physically and emotionally because we could not endure those tiny corpses, their coldness and their silence.

Eventually I fell into a restless sleep, but something disturbed me and I woke suddenly. It was completely dark and I could not see a thing. *I have gone blind*, I thought with a stab of fear. There was a smell of decay in my nostrils. *I am dead and in the grave.* I could not move, not even to bring my hand to my face to check if I could see it.

There was someone in the room. I could sense his presence. If it was a thief he had chosen the wrong house. The only things of value were my stories and they were inside my head and a meagre haul at best.

I could see nothing else, but I could discern a shape, wraith-like and insubstantial as though only partly formed, and a sound began to come from it, a muttering which was hard to catch, an ancient version of Japanese, words with a hollow ring, as if they had been spoken centuries before and had been hanging in the air waiting for an ear to receive them. They latched on to me like worms and one by one burrowed into my brain.

Here they burst into full form: the wailing of impaled infants, the shrieking of women raped and then burned alive, the cruelty of men far from home, away from all restraint on their bestial nature, inflicting on others what they themselves fled from. They had been hardened against their own grief; why should they feel the suffering of those they had been told were their enemies?

As the words fed on me my visitant began to solidify. I lay in blackness, unsure if I was alive or dead, while he spoke more clearly and became more real. I knew him; I recognised the words he spoke; it was the monk, Keinen.

There are no Buddhas, there are no gods, there is no heaven. Only this hell that we call the world.

Pray for me, oh pray for me!

My terror did not exactly abate but these last words intrigued and thrilled me. It was just like a Nō play: the main character had committed or witnessed a terrible crime and could not move on after death but must hover between the worlds until recognition and reparation happened and the spirit was released.

Keinen and his diary had been waiting for someone like me.

He came closer and leaned over me, three hundred years of the grave hanging around him.

Tell my story. Storyteller, tell my story.

The whole room turned cold. Outside Aka began to howl. Tae stirred beside me.

Tae	What's wrong? It's got so cold.
Sei	I had a bad dream.
Tae	Mmm.

As she snuggled against me, I checked my vision. I could see her vague shape in the darkness. I could no longer see Keinen. I put my arms around her. I could move again. I was filled with gratitude to my wife that she was warm and she was alive.

KEINEN'S VISITATION REMAINED vividly in my mind but I had the two versions of my article to write and for the next few days I concentrated on them. I was rewriting and repolishing for the fourth or fifth time when I received a note from my newspaper friend to say he had passed on the story I had given him to the editor of one of the new literary magazines, *Modern Days*. 'The author' was asked to get in touch directly.

Shigure received this news with her usual doubtful frown but went off to meet the editor and came back scowling even more to say they liked the story and were going to run it the following week.

Sei	That's wonderful!
Tae	Are they going to pay you?
Shigure	They offered four yen.

Sei   Not bad! So why are you looking so depressed?

Shigure   It's so poorly written. I can do so much better. If only I could take it back and rewrite it. Everyone's going to read it and comment on it. I can't bear it.

Sei   I don't suppose that many people will see it – the circulation is not huge.

Tae   You can withdraw it if it's so painful.

Shigure   No! I want to be published. I can't believe my story is going to appear in a magazine. I want people to read it, but I don't, at the same time.

Tae   Living with one writer is bad enough, living with two is going to be impossible.

Teru   Four yen is more than I get for a shawl, which takes a lot longer than a story and I have to pay for the wool.

Shigure   Your shawls are beautiful, every stitch perfect; there is nothing to discuss or review about them.

Teru   Some people like one colour, some prefer another. I can't please everyone and nor can you. As soon as I have finished one I immediately start on the next.

Shigure followed this sisterly advice and applied herself to her next piece of writing but she was still as restless as a cat in spring, could not eat or sleep and was vomiting on the morning the magazine came out. Tae went to buy some copies and we all admired the story, which appeared under the name of Akabane Shigure (she had been persuaded to use the family name in the interests of publicity). Shigure looked at it with white face and shaking hands.

Shigure   It's so far at the back! No one's going to see it!

Tae   So you don't need to worry about any criticism.

But one person who did see it was Shigure's husband, Ono Renzō.

I could say I had been putting off contacting Renzō to tell him that Shigure had not come home to look after her ailing father but had left him for good and wanted a divorce. The truth was that for the last few weeks I had not given him much thought at all. None of us had. Perhaps we hoped that he had just obligingly disappeared. I had always found him deeply uninteresting; we never had much to say to each other, and since Takayuki had paid my rent I no longer needed to ask him for a loan.

He came in the early evening when we were all at home. There was no time to pretend Shigure was out. He was well dressed in Western clothes and carried a leather bag containing gifts of sake, dried seaweed and so on, and a copy of *Modern Days*.

Renzō   I'm sorry I haven't come sooner, Master. You will think me a very poor son-in-law. I've been negotiating an important business deal. It's all finalised now, very satisfactory. You are looking well – you are quite recovered, I hope?
Sei   Thank you, yes.
Shigure   But not completely better yet, are you, Father? You still need nursing. And next week my sister is coming with her two little boys, so I need to stay a little longer to help Mother.
Renzō   Who is he?
Shigure   Who is who?
Renzō   The boy in your story, your secret lover?
Shigure   You read my story?

Renzō   Of course I did! I don't know how many people have told me about it. 'Isn't this your wife, Mr Ono?' So who is he? I'm going to kill him! Making you hang around in the rain so you catch pneumonia!

Shigure   It's a story! I made it up!

Renzō   It's set in our district. There are shops and streets I recognise. Your parents are in it. It has to be real!

Shigure   You don't know the first thing about writing.

Renzō   I may not know about writing but I do know about marriage. A woman's place is with her husband. You should be looking after the house and having children. Then you wouldn't have the time to indulge in scribbling. Get your things. I'm taking you home.

Shigure   I am not coming home, now or ever. I want a divorce.

Renzō   But you love me. You wrote in the story – it's your husband you love, you just hadn't realised it. I want you to come home and realise that you love me while we still have time to make children, before you get sick and die, before it's too late.

Shigure   It's not about you! You are not the husband! I made it all up!

Renzō   You don't love me? You want a divorce?

Shigure   I want to write. I don't want to waste my time on other things. I'm sorry. We should never have got married.

Renzō   But I love you. I didn't realise how much until you left. And when I read the story I thought you were trying to tell me something.

Shigure   I wasn't. I wasn't thinking about you at all. For the last time, I was making it up. Please don't cry. I don't want to feel sorry for you. Don't think I hate you. I don't. Perhaps I could have learned to love you as a wife should but it was all too difficult. Every day I was cut in two, trying to do my duty as a wife, trying to find some time for myself so I could write down the lines that had been obsessing me. I finished a story; it has been published, but it was written in stolen time; I could have made it so much better. Look how my father lives with nothing to distract him from his work. My mother does everything for him, puts out his clothes in the morning, undresses him at night, cooks the meals, does the washing, keeps the house clean, chases away the creditors.

Renzō   This is what women do. Anyway, I don't have any creditors.

Shigure   People come to the house all day long, wanting to sell something, borrow money . . . but that's not the point. I can't be a writer and a wife.

Renzō   What can I say to make you stay with me?

Shigure   Nothing.

I was quite surprised at Renzō's display of emotion and I think we were all moved by his pleas, except Shigure, who had been speaking quickly and coldly and now stared at him dry-eyed. She had always looked such a gentle willowy girl, half the time off in another world, daydreaming, but underneath she was as hard as steel and stubborn too. Teru, whose eyes had filled with tears for her brother-in-law, was far more sentimental and easily swayed. I was afraid Renzō was going to call on me to exercise the tyranny of a father and order my daughter to go back to him but Tae came to my rescue.

Tae　　　There's a lot we need to talk about. Dear son-in-law, please don't think badly of us. We are grateful to you for so many things. If I had known our daughter was going to become a writer I would have kept her at home. It is not easy being married to someone whose first love and first loyalty are to their stories. But that's the way artists are, blind and deaf to the people around them. Maybe that's the way they are born but they will certainly never change. My father, father-in-law and husband have all been like that. I should not be surprised to have a daughter who is the same.

Renzō　　　But once she has children she will give up this idea, won't she?

Shigure　　　I don't want to have children!

Renzō　　　What if I hire more maids?

Shigure　　　And who is going to supervise them?

Renzō　　　We could get a housekeeper – I am sure I have an old aunt or cousin somewhere.

Shigure　　　Please, just divorce me.

Tae　　　Let's not act in haste. Go home now, Renzō. My husband will come and discuss things with you in a few days.

Renzō was a handsome man in a rather frog-like way but his looks relied largely on his confident manner. Now, completely deflated, he was almost ugly. He got to his feet, grabbed the sake bottle he had brought and tucked it under his arm. He seemed about to seize Shigure in the same way and drag her off with him. At that moment I saw the bully who lay beneath the surface. I knew I could never send her back to him and I resigned myself to the fact that my youngest daughter was going to be divorced.

THE FOLLOWING WEEK the theatres closed for the seasonal break, Kyu was taken by Sakutarō to his summer house in Akane, and Kat'chan went off to climb Mount Yari. My oldest daughter, Yuri, and our grandsons, Fusao and Sojirō, came to stay with us. Fusao took after his father; even at six years old he was active and opinionated. Soji, as Tae had said, was the image of Tatsuo, the boy we had lost, sweet-natured, funny and already making up stories about his toys, Aka, things he saw in the street, even the pans and ladles in the kitchen.

He awakened all the grief, but also all the joy, of our son's short life and death. The first day just watching him brought tears to my eyes. Of course I did not want to frighten him by crying in front of him, but that night, after everyone else was asleep, I could not hold in any longer the tears I had hardly shed over fourteen years. My wife wept too and we held each other closely, and one thing led to another, making her very happy and, I must admit, me too.

Why had I denied us this sweet pleasure for so long? I entered a stage of renewed youth, and devoted a large part of my day to devising strategies so I might be alone with my wife, not easy with such a full house. My stories for once took second place and if I sometimes let my fantasies replace my wife with another, younger woman, the heroine of my tale, no one knew that but me.

It grew hotter and hotter. Street vendors called out through the day, *Ice! Watermelon!* Aka lay panting, hardly moving. The atmosphere in the house was lively and happy, although I was worried about our middle daughter, Teru. She often had tears in her eyes, and was visibly losing weight. *Her* husband had not come around to demand her back. In fact I'd heard he had gone away for the summer with Yūdai. Her life was being wasted through no fault of her own and I could see from the way she took care of Yuri's little boys that she longed to be a mother.

We would have to start looking for another husband. I began going through all the unmarried or widowed men of my acquaintance and Tae put the word out on her old milk network. It was a subject we often talked about at night, and we had this conversation shortly before O-Bon, the Festival of the Dead.

Sei   I could try another one of my disciples but Teru says she won't marry a performer of any kind. Maybe we should advertise? I've noticed people put a few lines in the newspapers, listing the virtues and accomplishments of their daughters and the qualities they are looking for in a son-in-law.

Tae   That seems a little desperate. Someone suggested Chie's young lodger, Mr Okuda. Apparently he isn't married and he's lived in France, so he's probably broad-minded. You like him, don't you?

Sei   I do like him, but he wouldn't be suitable at all.

Tae   Give me one good reason.

Sei   It would be like Tensa all over again. He's in love with someone else.

Tae   With another man?

Sei   No, no, with a woman. He wants to marry her.

Tae   Is that true? Or is it just something you made up?

Sei   It's true. I guarantee he will ask her to marry him before long. She will hear him talk at a meeting and on the way home they will linger under the willow trees, the moon shining on the water, night insects chirping, the first hint of autumn in the air. He will woo her with French poetry.

Tae   That's so romantic! Is this the new story you are writing?

Sei   Maybe I will use some of it, but it is basically true.

Tae   It's strange how suddenly everyone is talking about love and romance. Even we have become quite romantic at our age.

Sei   Yes, we have.

Tae   I'm glad, aren't you?

Sei   Yes.

And I was overcome by the need to prove it. It didn't take away the problem of a husband for Teru but it did make me forget it for a while.

At O-Bon we visited the family graves at our neighbourhood temple, offered fruit and flowers, rice and sake, to our beloved dead and then went down to the river to light lanterns and set them afloat. The children were made solemn by the knowledge that everyone would die but were comforted by the fact that death did not separate us from our families. We could come back and visit them and we would never be forgotten.

The women went home with the children but I stayed by the water for a little longer, watching the tiny lights float away on the tide, hearing the tearful farewells (and some not so tearful, rather cheery in fact due to large amounts of alcohol) of those left on the bank. Aka sat beside me, his eyes grave and dark, his nose twitching. There was a damp smell from the river as the mud became exposed and then Aka growled and the smell worsened into the stench of decay.

Everything around me went black, suddenly and completely as though all light had been extinguished from the world; candles, lanterns, stars, moon were wiped out. I could not move. Slowly Keinen took shape in front of me. He was hardly more than a skeleton, his skin stretched like rotting silk over his blackened bones. His hair and nails were long, as if they still persisted in growing, and a wispy beard hung from his chin. At first I thought he had no eyes but he turned his skull-like head towards me and I saw them glitter like tiny pinpoints of light from deep in the sockets. He laid one bony hand on my arm and I felt the weight press me down into the earth. Despite the heat I was freezing.

Yet I was not as frightened as I had been last time. I knew I was not blind or paralysed or in the grave; I was in Keinen's world, where only his need to be heard existed. I admired him for his determination, which not even death and three centuries had been able to diminish, as well as the courage and compassion of his writing. I couldn't deny that for a storyteller there was something rather special about being chosen by a ghost. But he was going to make impossible demands on me that I was not sure I could satisfy.

He spoke as before in fragments, begging me to bring his words to light, to disclose the truth, telling me I was his only hope. There was much I wanted to say in reply, but I could not move my lips. I thought about the other demands on me, the *yose* hall waiting for me in a month, Takayuki expecting me to do something in return for my rent, the ever-growing queue of my own stories. I argued silently that audiences did not want to be made to feel guilty or to be obliged to atone for the crimes of the past, that history only interested them if it was glorious and flattering, that I was not a hero, or a political activist. I was just a middle-aged storyteller. I did not deal in truth, I dealt only in lies.

Keinen's hand pressed down on me more heavily. Through it I felt all the weight of the dead, the massacred, the tortured, those killed without pity or remorse. And something within me sparked. I did not think I could ever put into words the horrors I had glimpsed, yet surely there was a way – perhaps a satire, a black comedy ... I heard Tensa's voice distinctly say, *The Hill of Ears* ... I would need a setting ... characters ... that part of my brain where inspiration germinated had gone into the state of blank feverishness which I knew meant something was about to be born.

A sound from the real world penetrated the dense blackness, a frantic, urgent howling. Aka. It could only mean one thing – and not the arrival of his master's great idea. A few seconds later there was a grinding roar, buildings rattled, people shouted in shock and surprise. As my hearing returned so did my sight. The real world flashed in and out of my darkened mind like lightning. The river rippled and surged before my eyes as the earth's shaking reversed the movement of the tide. Yet Keinen still held me imprisoned.

Sei	It's an earthquake! A big one!
Keinen	Nature is less cruel than man.
Sei	Let me go. I must go home.
Aka	*Roooo arooo rooo.*
Keinen	Do you promise?
Sei	Yes, yes, I promise.

Keinen released me, dissolving into the gritty air, and with a clap like thunder the world reassembled itself around me.

Fires were already breaking out, dust and smoke swirling around me as I hurried home, but the wind was blowing towards the river, which saved our district from serious damage, apart from the burial ground, where stones were overthrown and graves broken open. The smell of death hung over the city all summer, the background to the story I now began to write: 'The History of a Nose'.

SEPTEMBER WAS APPROACHING, Kat'chan returned from the mountains and took Yuri and the boys home, and the first day of my booking loomed ever closer. I had finished 'The History of a Nose' but I was rather uneasy about presenting it. It was quite unlike anything I had done before. I thought Keinen might approve of it but I was not sure any living audience would. My other great story, which I envisaged telling over several days, was far from complete. I had my characters and I had begun to set them in motion but I had no idea where they were going or what would happen to them. I had to get something else together, so I turned to Satoshi and his store of French literature.

I spent many hours over the summer talking to Satoshi and became very fond of him. I would have liked him as a son-in-law and often wondered if I should enlighten him about Michi's relationship with Takayuki, of which he seemed completely unaware. However the time was never quite right.

Michi and Takayuki had become more discreet. I did not see them together. If they met it must be at a teahouse with private rooms like the place where I had interviewed Kyu, or in Takayuki's house. Only Kyu's revelations kept me from thinking I had imagined the whole thing and invented out of a single moment an entire love affair. All in all it seemed better to say nothing.

Satoshi was teaching French both at the language academy and to a few private pupils. He was on the brink of a promising career. Despite being so busy he had found time to translate some short stories for me – we decided stories would be simpler than a whole novel. They were by Guy de Maupassant, whom Satoshi and I affectionately called Monsieur Guy, very new and modern; we did not think anyone in Tokyo would know them. They took place against the backdrop of a recent war between two neighbouring European countries, France and Prussia, which even though on the other side of the world were not unlike Japan and Korea. Satoshi and I had some amusing discussions about which might be which. By September I had adapted (freely) and rehearsed two of them. One I called 'Princess Pig' and the other 'Two Friends'.

Princess Pig was the nickname I gave to a plump former geisha travelling with various officials and their wives, and two nuns, in some occupied territory. They are detained by a commanding officer of the enemy forces (Prussian in the original story but in my new version perhaps Korean) who will not let them progress unless Princess Pig agrees to sleep with him. She declines; she is on her way to be married and has given up her old way of life. Moreover, the officer is not attractive to her. At first her companions are outraged on her behalf but gradually they come to blame her for their continued detention and try to persuade her to give in; even the nuns preach that one person should sacrifice herself for the sake of mankind, like the rabbit that jumped into the cooking pot to feed the Buddha. After all, it is just one more man. What difference can it make to her after so many? Princess Pig complies, with many tears, and they are allowed to continue on their way, but now the others despise her as a prostitute, and when her husband-to-be hears the rumours he calls off the wedding.

It all took place in the snow, which is always pleasing to describe. I love winter stories, especially on hot autumn evenings.

The second story was also set during the Franco–Prussian war. Satoshi had tried to explain to me the struggles for power in Europe and we concluded there could be parallels with our own country's rise among Asian nations. Again I intimated that the occupying forces might be Korean. The two friends are passionate fishermen, prevented from pursuing their favourite pastime by the circumstances of war. They receive a password to get through their own military lines, spend the day on the bank of their beloved river, and are rewarded by a splendid catch. They philosophise about the nature and futility of war but are finally arrested by the enemy and, when they refuse to divulge the password, are shot on the orders of the occupying officer, a cruel and brutal man. The story ends with this officer having the fish fried alive.

I added a few jokes and puns throughout, laughter in the face of death, which I had found never failed to move an audience.

I was all too aware of my debt to Takayuki, which I could not afford to repay as I still owed the bookseller for Keinen's diary. I hoped these oblique references would satisfy him and be enough to settle our score.

I was extremely nervous the first evening. The hall, the Kiharatei in Nihonbashi, was decorated with lanterns and flowers; it was completely full and the atmosphere was merry. Rinjirō had worked hard to drum up interest and I suppose my name had some sort of pulling power. Shigure and Teru both attended and Satoshi was there too, sitting just behind them. The audience welcomed me with expectant faces and received my meagre offerings from the start with laughter, tears and applause.

My nervousness disappeared and I began to enjoy myself. How I loved this! Why had I put off performing for so long? Retirement? Forget it! I would go on till I died on stage, like my father.

I was halfway through the second story when I noticed Takayuki standing at the back, partly hidden behind a pillar. I could see enough of his face to guess he was unmoved by my art. His stern expression rather dampened my ebullience, but I don't think the audience noticed. By the end of the story they were hanging on every word in complete silence. A collective gasp of horror went up at the friends' death and several people dabbed their eyes on their sleeves.

Rinjirō expressed his delight in his usual extravagant way, adding that his only concern was that the evening was too short. I should add at least one more story, two if possible. I basked in praise from the audience, chatted to some old colleagues, exchanging more jokes and puns, introduced Satoshi all round as the source of the French stories and was preparing to go off to a teahouse with them when Takayuki approached and indicated he wanted to speak to me in private.

I told my friends I would join them later. My daughters went home to convey my success to their mother (Tae rarely came to my perfomances, saying they made her too nervous). The hall emptied. Rinjirō hovered, eager to close up. Takayuki made an impatient gesture and led me outside.

There was a dark narrow alley alongside the hall and when we stepped into it two men were standing in the shadows. They looked like workmen with bare arms, leggings and split-toed boots, but the light glinted on the pictures on their skin. They did not say anything, ducked their heads to Takayuki, and waited.

I was still elated and foolishly expected compliments from Takayuki, but of course did not get any.

Takayuki　　　It won't do at all. Princess Pig having to sleep with a foreign officer – it's an insult to the great Saigō!

Sei　　　Saigō? I don't mention Saigō. I know you and your group Black Ocean admire him greatly but it's not about him at all.

Takayuki　　　Princess Pig was the nickname of Saigō's favourite geisha. Don't tell me you didn't know that!

Sei　　　I didn't!

Takayuki　　　Well, you'll have to change it. Call her something else. But I don't like the story anyway. Is the officer meant to be Korean? Koreans don't have uniforms as you described. And are you suggesting Japan is occupied by a Korean army? That's impossible and it verges on treason.

Sei　　　The audience liked it.

119

Takayuki   And the second one. Are the two men who go fishing Japanese?

Sei   Well, naturally they are French, really, but I have transposed the story.

Takayuki   So that officer is also Korean? And again Japan is the occupied country?

Sei   The friends are the heroes of the story.

Takayuki   Not in my opinion. There is something despicable about them. All that whining about the futility of war. The officer is much more admirable. Make him Japanese.

Sei   But his cruelty . . . ?

Takayuki   Better to be cruel than weak.

Sei   I'm sorry. It's obviously not possible for me to meet your needs. I'll pay you back your money.

Takayuki   We had an agreement. You gave me your word.

Sei   I don't remember giving you my word as such. I had too much to drink . . .

Takayuki   *They* know who you are. *They* know where you live.

He turned abruptly and walked away. The men looked me straight in the face in an intimidating manner and followed him. One of them laughed, high-pitched, like a woman.

I was left in the alley alone and deflated. The sounds and smells of the city rose and fell around me, yet I felt I was at the bottom of a deep, dark well. I was cold. I'd never thought of myself as being a coward but up to that point in my life I had never faced any physical threat. Now I felt a kind of dread invade me. Someone came round the corner, making me jump in fright. It was my manager.

Rinjirō   Master? What are you doing here? Everyone's waiting for you.

Sei   How much money do we have?

Rinjirō   Don't worry about money. The refreshments are all on the house and you'll earn plenty in the next few weeks.

Sei   I need fifty yen immediately.

Rinjirō   The truth is, at the moment we are in debt. We always are at the beginning of a season – hiring the hall, decorations, publicity. But tonight was a success; we'll soon be fine.

Sei   I need to settle a personal debt at once.

Rinjirō   I don't think I can possibly raise another fifty right now. It's a lot of money. Maybe in a few weeks.

Sei   Then I will have to change the stories. Or write new ones.

Rinjirō   But people loved them and you told them brilliantly. I've advertised them as new stories based on the most up-to-date French literature. You have another performance tomorrow. Really, there is no time to rewrite and rehearse. Believe me, the stories are fine.

I allowed him to lead me off to the teahouse, where I drank too much so that when I finally got home and lay down the futon swayed and rolled like a fragile boat on a deep ocean. Tae went straight to sleep, every now and then emitting a tiny snore but I remained restless and wakeful. In the end I got up, lit a lamp, went into my study and sat thinking about my stories. I was not sure I could alter them to suit Takayuki – not out of any great sense of integrity or courage but simply because once the story was created, that was the way it was. It could be improved, certainly, refined through constant performance, but not changed in essence. I liked the name Princess Pig – who apart from Takayuki would know about Saigō's favourite geisha, and anyway, didn't that add another, melancholy dimension? Still, I thought after a while, I could sacrifice that, call her Roly Poly or Tub of Lard. And I could state clearly that both stories took place in France. I would abandon all references, hinted or otherwise, to Korea. That would probably also be more honourable towards the author, Monsieur Guy, from whom I was stealing them.

Then there was the question of the third story. The only one I had written was 'The History of a Nose'. If Takayuki hadn't liked the first two, he was going to hate this one.

It was shortly before dawn and throughout the city roosters were beginning to crow. Spots flickered before my eyes and I thought I could smell decay. The idea of another visitation from Keinen disturbed me. I would not break my promise to the dead. My annoyance with Takayuki increased. Who was he to think he could dictate to me? He had not even thought to compliment me on my performance. He had spoiled my enjoyment of my success. What he was asking me to do was ignoble. I would not be ordered around by him. The only commands I listened to were from my stories. My only loyalty was to them.

I stumbled back to bed. My head was throbbing and my mouth was dry. I wanted nothing more than to burrow into my wife's warm body but emotion and alcohol had rendered me incapable and I only succeeded in annoying her.

THE NEXT DAY crawled slowly by. I reworked the two French stories, renamed Princess Pig Roly Poly, and practised 'The History of a Nose'. I felt unwell most of the day but as the performance approached the familiar excitement and anticipation began to take hold of me and by the time I walked on stage and took my place on my striped silk cushion I was filled with a febrile energy that bordered on recklessness.

Rinjirō told me all the seats had been sold; if Takayuki or his tatooed men were in the audience I did not see them.

I did however catch sight of Jack Green, whose attendance gave me a great deal of pleasure. Throughout the first two stories I kept glancing towards him and I was increasingly gratified at his reactions. He seemed completely engaged, laughing, and even crying, unlike certain of my colleagues, also there, who affected their usual distant critical demeanour, tapping their fingers together and pursing their mouths. I tried not to look at them and in the interval sent Rinjirō to find Jack Green and invite him to my dressing-room.

He was a tall man with a long thin nose and light eyes of a colour between grey and green, like stones in a riverbed. He had an extremely well shaped mouth, an important attribute for a storyteller, and the same mobility of expression as my son-in-law Tensa. He was wearing trousers of a soft fawn material and a frilled white shirt with a scarf tied at his neck under a short Japanese jacket with the Chinese character for 'green' embroidered on the sleeves and back. I didn't know then that it was the meaning of his name.

I was drinking cold barley tea and poured him a cup. He drank a little and then commented on the Guy de Maupassant stories, which he had heard of but not read. He thought they translated well into Japanese. I played the role of the magnanimous older artist and thanked him for putting the idea of French material in my head with his marvellous rendition of Joan of Arc, and told him about Satoshi. He adopted the corresponding role gracefully, expressing his gratitude that I, the Master, should have come to listen to him.

Jack Green   So what is in store for us next? More de Maupassant?

Sei   Something I have written myself. This will be the first time I've tried it out. I'll look forward to hearing your opinion afterwards.

He took a small silver flask from his trouser pocket, unscrewed the cap and poured the contents into the two teacups.

Jack Green   A little toast to your success, Master.

He swallowed his in one gulp and I did the same. It was whisky, which I had tasted on a few occasions, and it immediately increased my reckless mood. The sound of the wooden clappers warned us that the second half of the performance was about to begin. Jack Green took his leave and I picked up my fan and my handtowel, entered the hall, knelt down on my cushion and began.

The History of a Nose

Some years ago I went to Kyoto. I had been invited to a storytelling festival in Osaka *(opportunity to use the Osaka dialect)* and after spending several days exchanging stories, eating oysters and clams, and drinking rather more than I should, I decided I needed some spiritual cleansing and would go and visit the great temples and shrines of the old capital. It was at the end of autumn; the last of the red and yellow leaves were falling and the nights were frosty. On the third day the city was enveloped in a heavy white fog and, though it was very cold, I took advantage of the unusual weather to view the sights as they are rarely seen. The Five-Storey Pagoda seemed to disappear into heaven, the Golden Pavilion shone with an unearthly light, Chion'in was like a haunted mansion, moisture dripping like tears from the faces of statues, and the verandah at Kiyomizudera extended over the void. All sound was muffled. Not even a crow called.

I was the only person around apart from priests carrying out their sacred duties. I heard the sound of their footsteps, the ringing of a bell; they loomed like ghosts out of the all-enveloping whiteness and then disappeared into it again. I thought how like our lives this seemed. We came from blankness, existed for our little moment and then disappeared again.

Occupied with such sombre thoughts, I stumbled into a low bamboo fence which encircled a small mound, half-buried in wild grass and sedge. Wondering what it might be, I walked around it until I came to a faded sign which I deciphered as reading: *The Hill of Ears.*

I could not remember ever being here before, though I had been to Kyoto numerous times, and my curiosity was aroused by this name, which sounded at first poetic, like the Listening Hill, very appropriate for the hushed atmosphere that hung like the mist, but then more sinister. There was a temple nearby and there I found a priest intoning a long prayer before a wooden Buddha, so old it might have been carved in the lifetime of Shaka, the holy saint, himself. The whole place was dilapidated, the floorboards rotting, the beams riddled with wormholes, the hangings made lacy by moths and mice. Even the bowl which the priest struck several times during his interminable prayer emitted a dull cracked sound.

Eventually he finished and noticed me with a start. His mouth dropped open and his wrinkled ivory-coloured flesh shuddered. I realised the silence of my appearance out of the white mist had made him believe I was a phantom, yet he did not seem unduly surprised, as though the dead often visited him. I spoke to reassure him and asked the name of the temple and the significance of the small mound, the Hill of Ears.

His eyes turned in the direction of the donation bowl, which was completely empty, devoid even of the few small coins usually left in such receptacles to encourage the generous spirited. I took a couple of *rin* from my purse and tossed them in. They made a miserable tinkle and lay there looking forlorn.

'Long, long ago,' the priest said, 'it was the custom to offer an ear as a sign of devotion to the gods and to ensure one's prayers were answered.'

I had never heard of such a custom and I was a little incredulous.

'Come,' he said. 'I'll show you.' He led me down the side of the temple to a small shrine where a rusty knife lay on a brown-stained boulder. In front of it was a box, air-tight, the sort used to store precious, perishable objects. He opened the box solemnly and allowed me to peer inside. In it lay a shrivelled object that ressembled nothing so much as a pickled plum.

'This is the knife that was used,' said the old priest. 'That reddish colour is blood and that is an ear, preserved for centuries.'

The knife did not look so very old and the 'blood' was obviously rust. As for the 'ear', well, it looked nothing like an ear, no matter how long preserved. I peered at it closely.

'That is a nose!' I exclaimed.

'No, it is an ear,' he said firmly. 'Who would cut off his own nose? An ear doesn't matter. You've got two, you can spare one if you're devoted enough.'

I thought about that. I am very fond of my fine appendage. It is quite a wonderful organ, extremely sensitive to smell, and the means by which air goes in and out of my lungs. If it becomes blocked with winter colds or summer hay fever my whole being suffers. It is almost certainly my second favourite appendage. Certainly I would never voluntarily remove it from my body. Yet the more I studied the sad shrivelled thing in the box, the less I believed the priest.

'I can see the nostrils. There are two holes. An ear would only have one.'

'It only has one when fixed to the head, but once it is cut off it has two.'

This made no sense to me but the old man was becoming tetchy, so I thanked him and left that mournful place to make my way home. However the mist was so thick I soon became lost and there was not a soul around to seek help from. I was standing at a crossroads, wondering which of the three muddy options I should take, each of them ending in a blank wall of vapour, when I sensed someone approaching behind me and turned to see a nose emerging from the mist.

I waited for the rest of the face to follow but nothing came. Just the nose, hanging in the air, roughly where it would have been attached to a man slightly taller than myself. It looked as if it had just been severed. It was bleeding a little and tags of muscle and gristle quivered as it spoke. I suppose you will find it hard to believe that a nose can utter words, but watch my fine appendage and see the delicate movements it makes as I speak. You will find it easy to understand. And I understood the Nose's speech despite it being, well, nasal. As for what language the Nose spoke, the dead all speak one language and it is one we all understand.

'That idiot!' the Nose said, referring no doubt to the old priest. 'He has been telling the same lie for years.'

'I knew you were not an ear,' I said with, under the circumstances, an absurd feeling of justification.

'You judged for yourself with your own eyes what you saw,' replied the Nose, 'while most people believe whatever they are told. This mound is an embarrassment to Buddhist priests who adhere to their doctrine of no harm. At first they claimed that under the mound lay ears taken from vanquished but valiant enemies for whom the monument was erected and prayers offered daily, then even that seemed too brutal. That senile old fellow invented the idea of the willing sacrifice, persuaded an antiques dealer to donate the knife, stained the stone with red dye . . . I will tell you what lies under that unholy mound: tens of thousands of noses cut from the dead and the living – soldiers, peasants, monks, men, women – in a gruesome offering to Hideyoshi, the great general and unifier of Japan, but the Butcher of Korea.'

My audience had been hanging spellbound on every word but at this point in my story there was a disturbance at the back of the hall and someone shouted something I could not hear but which was certainly not laudatory. I saw Rinjirō move swiftly towards the heckler and I pressed on.

'So you are Korean?' I addressed the Nose.

'Yes, I am from a man born in Sachon, a monk, seized from a temple. A Japanese soldier cut me off while I still lived. Hundreds of noses that day were put in great barrels of brine, the salt stripping away all other smells, but a physician, the monk Keinen, took me away and mummified me with some secret art. I was sealed in an air-tight box and offered to the temple, so I did not moulder away into dust with the other thousands under the Hill of Ears.

'Why were so many noses collected?'

'We were the tally of the dead, not as heavy as heads and easier to count than ears. Soldiers were paid a bonus, commanders boosted their battle figures, Hideyoshi triumphed in his victory.'

From outside the hall came more shouting and banging on the doors, which Rinjirō had shut and locked. A murmur of unrest passed through the audience. I was afraid I was losing them. I lowered my voice to a whisper. Everyone leaned forward, straining to hear.

It was icy cold at the crossroads. The fog had not lessened – if anything it was thicker. The Nose said, 'I will show you the way. I will be your guide,' and it accompanied me to my lodging place. Since then it has been at my side day and night. It is here now. Do you see it?'

I turned to look at the Nose and the audience gasped. I spoke directly and softly to it. 'I have done what you asked of me. I have told your story. Now begone and rest in peace.'

My eyes followed the Nose's departure. The hall was silent for a full minute. I smiled and bowed, fanning my face with a deep sigh of relief. Then I sat up suddenly, turned my gaze on one of the closest spectators and whispered to him, 'Don't be afraid if the Nose has attached itself to you. It just wants you to listen to its story.'

THERE WERE SEVERAL gasps as I made the traditional
farewell – *And now I leave you in the capable hands of
the next story.* Then for a moment there was silence, followed
by some shouts of approval and prolonged clapping, but the
audience did not hang around to congratulate me as they had
the previous night and the atmosphere was quite different.
I had no doubt my story had been moving but perhaps it had
demanded a little too much from my listeners. Rinjirō made an
astonished face at me, as if to say, *Where did that come from?*
He opened the doors, and most people trickled out quietly.
Only Jack Green remained in the hall.

Jack   Congratulations! That was quite a tale. I could
almost see the Nose beside you. Really, no one can tell a story
like you.

Sei   Do you think they liked it? They've all left in a hurry!

Jack   It will linger in their minds, I believe. It was very powerful.

Sei   It should be. If the dead can't tell a good story, who can?

Jack laughed, as if he understood what I meant. I was suddenly exhausted; the sleepless night and the tension of telling the ghost story had left me drained. I apologised to Jack – I would have liked to go somewhere and talk with him, but I had to go home. He asked where I lived and said he would walk with me as it was on the way to his place in Tsukiji. Rinjirō, who was cleaning up the hall, called out that he would come round in the morning.

It was a calm autumn night, moonless, so the stars could be seen clearly. The teahouses and boats along the river were still busy, their lights spilling on the water setting up fractured reflections. Jack was talkative, which was lucky, as I had run out of words. He told me about himself, his life as a child in Yokohama, his family's distress at his theatrical efforts, how he thought he should do something more acceptable to them but storytelling was what he loved and he feared he was hopelessly addicted to it. We attracted quite a few stares as we walked along side by side, and he was constantly propositioned by the teahouse girls, who collapsed in giggles when he replied in fluent local slang.

To be honest it was the first time I had walked alongside a foreigner and chatted as with a friend. I kept thinking he would not understand, that I should simplify my speech. His appearance was so different, his language so familiar. It was intriguing and attractive but also rather affronting. I wished I could speak a foreign language so well. I wondered if it was too late to start learning English, or maybe Satoshi would teach me French.

We left the brightly lit path along the river and walked into a poorer district of low-roofed houses, broken verandahs and sagging eaves. It was much darker here and we were picking our way carefully over the uneven surface when two figures emerged from the shadows in front of us, seeming to rise almost out of the ground. They did not say anything, nor did they give us time to react. Ignoring Jack, as though their eyes were not capable of seeing a foreigner, one of them swiftly seized my arms and pinioned them behind my back, while the other began to beat me systematically from head to groin.

I struggled, yelling out in shock and surprise, twisting my head, trying to avoid the blows. Jack punched the man hitting me, catching him low in the back, in the kidney, and as he doubled over, Jack delivered a crunching blow to the side of the man's head. Before he could recover, Jack had his hands around the neck of the other man, cutting off his windpipe until he loosened his grip on me. As he struggled away, Jack spun him round and kneed him in the groin.

Jack yelled in surprise at the exact moment that my sense of smell awoke and told me this was not a man but a woman. My legs were refusing to support me and I fell over, tripping up the man who was coming back at Jack. While he was off balance Jack was able to land another punch on his head, knocking him to the ground.

Jack pulled me to my feet, put my arm across his shoulder and half-carried, half-dragged me down the street.

No one followed us. I imagined Jack's defence of me was more than they expected. We did not speak until we came to the front of my house. Aka leaped up from a sound sleep, yelped at me and began to bark at Jack in a new and savage way I had never heard before. I tried to quieten him.

Jack   They really didn't like the story! I've heard of hostile audiences but that was extreme! I think one of them was a woman. I've never punched a woman before.

Sei   Yes, one was. A very frightening woman.

Jack   You're bleeding. I hope you are not badly hurt.

Sei   My nose might be broken. How about you?

Jack   My fist hurts a bit. I must have landed quite a punch.

Sei   Thank you. You were very effective.

Jack   I've done a bit of boxing and wrestling. We were lucky they weren't using knives. Do you have any idea who they were?

Of course I did. They were Takayuki's thugs. *They know who you are*, he had said. They had not intended to kill me – if they had, they would have used knives and I would now be bleeding to death in the alley; the beating had been to teach me a lesson, to intimidate me. But I did not want to tell Jack this yet.

I was trembling, wild with anger and tearful at the same time. My nose was throbbing and my left side hurt when I breathed.

Aka's barking had roused my family. My wife came to the door, followed by Teru and Shigure, both in nightclothes, their hair loose. Any surprise they might have felt at seeing the Englishman was overtaken by their shock and concern for me.

Jack helped me inside, kicking off his shoes in the entrance. Teru ran to get cloths from the kitchen. My wife showed Jack the room where she had spread out the bedding and fetched a back rest so I could sit up. I protested, as I did not want to get blood on the quilt or the tatami, but they ignored me and placed me down on the futon. Teru began to wash away the blood and she and Tae assessed the damage. Shigure looked anxiously from one to the other.

Shigure   Shall I fetch a doctor?
Tae   Run next door and ask Miss Itasaki to come over – that will be quicker.
Sei   No, no! Not her!
Tae   She's as good as any doctor. Go, Shigure.

I was terrified Takayuki would be with her and they would appear together but a few minutes later Michi arrived alone, a jacket thrown over her yukata, her hair pulled back in a European-style bun, her doctor's bag in her hand.

Michi   Master, what happened to you?
Jack   He was attacked after the performance. There had been some heckling earlier and two people were asked to leave. The manager will be able to describe them to the police.
Michi   Well, let's see. Where does it hurt the most?

She probed my face and my chest with an expert, not very gentle, touch.

135

Sei   Ahh! My nose, down this side.

Michi   Your nose is broken and possibly a rib too. Both should set by themselves. Breathing will be less painful if I bind up your middle, so please slip out of your clothes. And I'll stitch the cut on your cheek so it heals better.

She gave me some painkilling mixture and I sat half-naked while she wrapped a long cotton bandage tightly round the lower part of my chest and back and then deftly drew together the sides of the wound on my face with four stitches. The prick of the needle brought tears again to my eyes, not only from the pain but also from the pathos: an old man who had not been hit since childhood, surrounded by four women, three of them young and attractive. I wondered what Jack made of this scene and then I found myself wondering if he were married. Of course, given the perversity of human nature, if he was attracted to any one of them it would be Michi. He would join Satoshi and Takayuki in the competition for her affections. And then what would Takayuki do to him?

Even in this injured state I could not stop making up stories. I blamed the painkiller for making my mind wander. Then I was overcome by gratitude towards them all, to Jack Green for rescuing me, to my family for their loving concern . . . and to Michi. But though I felt grateful to her, it was tempered by mistrust. Her calm practicality, her deft use of the needle, her *fearlessness* reminded me of the hardness I had seen in her before that had made me think of murderesses. Yet even as I thought this, she was easing my pain, making me feel a deep need for her, an emotion close to love.

I PASSED A RESTLESS night and in the morning was weak and
feverish. Tae brought me a mirror to show me my black eyes
and swollen nose. I was unrecognisable. Purple bruises stained
my skin, spreading out from under the bandage like pulped
fruit. My mouth hurt too fiercely to eat; my teeth felt loose.
Obviously I would not be able to give much of a performance – I
could barely talk – but I was determined not to cancel. I did
not want to be silenced by Takayuki and I wanted people to
see what had been done to me.

Rinjirō turned up before midday. I thought he must have
somehow heard of the attack, but he hadn't, and the news

together with my battered appearance gave him such a shock he wept for a good five minutes, unable to speak.

Tae　　　Apparently you threw out some hecklers – it could have been them. You must go to the police.

Rinjirō　　　What I came to tell you was that we have been closed down – by the police. When I went to the hall this morning they'd stuck a notice on the door saying all perform-ances were cancelled. I went to the district office to complain and was told the content was unsuitable and unpatriotic.

Tae　　　Unpatriotic? They're just stories!

Rinjirō　　　It was 'The History of a Nose' that caused the problem. Oh, why didn't you let me hear it first? I would never have allowed you to take such a risk.

Sei　　　But it's true . . . an eyewitness account.

Rinjirō　　　It's a ghost story! How can it be an eyewitness account? Don't talk such nonsense. Anyway, whether it's true or not is completely irrelevant. We are closed down; we have no way to recoup our debts. It's a disaster.

Rinjirō had lost his usual respectful way of speaking and was openly angry with me. The shock of this, piled on top of all the other things, shamed me. I did not understand it. I was the victim of an attack yet I was the one who felt deeply ashamed.

Rinjirō wiped his eyes, sat in gloomy silence for a while and then said he would see if he could come to some agreement with our creditors.

Tae did not want to leave me so Teru went to the market in her place. Shigure sat with us for a while and then retired upstairs to write up her journal, saying she wanted to record events while they were still fresh in her mind. I imagined it would make a change from her usual subject matter, the daily record of her rather humdrum life. Apart from occasionally meeting some of her old friends, she hardly went out. She had taken over the storeroom in the rafters of the house and she spent her days there or in my study reading through my books and writing. The slight success of her first story lay in the past. She had not finished anything since. She was losing her looks, becoming thin and pale. It was a good thing she did not want to marry again, but what was to become of her? I was making myself tearful again.

Tae took my hand.

Tae	You feel very hot.
Sei	It must be a hot day.
Tae	No, it's quite cool, but you are burning.

She brought cold water and a cloth and sponged my face, neck and arms.

Sei   Thank you. I am sorry to have caused you so much trouble.

Tae   Is it something to do with the money, with the person who paid our rent?

Sei   In a way, yes.

Tae   I knew you were getting into something dangerous. You must tell the police. Rinjirō can identify your attackers.

Sei   I don't think going to the police will do any good.

Tae   What was the story that upset everyone so much?

I told her in halting sentences about the diary I had found while I was looking for books on Korea, its shocking and powerful descriptions, and its author, Keinen, whose account had been concealed for centuries but now demanded to be told. I wanted to tell her about Keinen's haunting presence and the promise he had extracted from me, but I was having enough problems speaking of what I knew to be real, without trying to explain the supernatural as well.

Tae   Why should you care so much about Korea? As far as I can see they need to be taught a lesson.

Sei   But why do you think that? When did you start having these ideas?

Tae   I don't know. It's what everybody thinks, isn't it? You read a bit here, a bit there. It influences you.

Sei   Exactly. The person who paid our rent wanted me to add my voice to that pervasive influence. And I felt an obligation to him, so I started researching the subject, but what I found was the diary and it opened my eyes. I realised I shouldn't do anything that would help lead us into an invasion, a war as terrible as Hideyoshi's which Keinen tells us the truth about.

Tae   Did you buy that book?

Sei   Yes.

Tae   How much?

Sei   Umm. Not that much. Forty yen.

Tae   I can't believe it! Cash?

Sei   I paid five in cash. I owe thirty-five.

Tae   I'll take it back. Where is it? Who sold it to you?

Sei   Kuruba Gozaemon.

Tae   I suppose it can wait a day or two. You poor old fool. Everyone liked the French stories. Why didn't you stick to them?

I did not tell her that even they had angered Takayuki. I closed my eyes. My head was aching. I could not sleep. Despite the laudanum Michi had left me, I kept having brutal memories, felt that grip on my arms that rendered me powerless (a woman's grip, which somehow made it worse), and heard my nose breaking.

Teru came back from the market; she and Tae were busying themselves in the kitchen when, not long after, Aka began barking in his new savage way and I heard Jack Green's voice outside. There was something about him, some foreign quality, that upset my dog. Perhaps it was his clothes or maybe Aka held Jack responsible for my misfortune.

After asking how I was feeling, Jack sat down next to me and Teru brought him a cup of tea and then sat down herself, smiling at him in a rather forward way. To my surprise Shigure emerged, holding her diary, and joined the circle. Usually she hid away from any visitors, saying she could not spare the time and she loathed small talk. She actually spoke to Jack, thanking him for assisting me. Both my daughters were regarding him with expectant eyes, as though he were a great performing bear.

Sei   Do you want to interview us about the incident?

Shigure	I could, couldn't I? That would make the entry more vivid.
Jack	Do you keep a diary?
Shigure	Yes. I write stories too, but they're not very good – though I did get one published, in *Modern Days*.
Jack	I would like to read it.

At that moment another visitor called out at the front door and Tae showed him in. It was Satoshi.

Tae	Mr Okuda has come to inquire after you.
Satoshi	I just heard of your misfortune. Miss Itasaki told me. She said she would call by later – she has gone to sit her exam today. How can such a terrible thing happen to you, such a respected man, such an artist? I hope it was not due to de Maupassant!
Sei	Let's blame Monsieur Guy. It was all his fault. What an appalling writer!
Satoshi	I admire the way you can make a joke out of it.
Sei	This is my source of French stories, Okuda Satoshi, and this is the English storyteller, Jack Green, who came to my rescue last night with a fine display of boxing in the English fashion.
Shigure	I wish I'd seen it.
Jack	The English fashion corrupted by Yokohama street fighting, I'm afraid. But I don't think anyone will be making complaints.
Teru	You must be very well known; I hope it won't be dangerous or harmful for you.
Jack	Your father is more famous than I am – we will

have to hope our fame protects us. I was warned by the police once. I made a few speeches about democracy and the rights of man, using examples from the history of English politics.

Satoshi   Really? I have been asked to give a lecture on a similar topic from the French perspective.

Shigure   Mr Jack had better go with you as your bodyguard.

Satoshi   Did they close you down?

Jack   Yes, until I changed my material. I had to go back to simple storytelling and give up politics. I suppose it was wisest. This country, which I consider my own, has a long way to go and many aspects of its government have to change, but it's not going to happen overnight. Trying to oppose the current regime is like the egg taking on the mountain; it's the egg that gets smashed. People demand democracy without really understanding what the word means. A lot of protest is more about resistance to new taxes than genuine concern about people's rights.

Satoshi   That's true – a real mix has gathered under the People's Rights banner: peasants who hate conscription, farmers who resent land tax, gamblers who've been declared outlaws, as well as genuine political progressives.

Shigure   We all want more freedom, and if we are asked to pay tax we should have a say in who imposes that tax – that is, who governs us.

Satoshi   Has there ever been progress without blood being shed? Both the English and the French executed their kings.

Teru   But our country cannot afford civil protests and unrest. We have to be united to become powerful and take our place among the nations of the world.

Satoshi   So the newspapers keep telling us. But we also have the chance to become a model of good government, one that does not seek power and influence through war but that sets an example to the rest of the world. The government has to listen to its people. We have a right to be heard.

Jack   If you say these things at your lecture you will certainly be closed down! Then all three of us will share the distinction.

Shigure   You could put it on your advertisements: *Closed by the Tokyo Police!*

We continued talking about politics and then moved on to literature and women writers in England and France. I was amazed at how animated my daughters were and could only put it down to the presence of the two young men. I took little part in the conversation and eventually Tae noticed my exhaustion and suggested our visitors should come back another day; they would always be welcome but now I needed to rest.

I lay in a semi-doze, fragments of the conversations swirling through my head, mingled with surprise that my daughters were so well informed and opinionated, fantasies about having an Englishman as a son-in-law, and suspicions that neither Teru nor Shigure would be averse.

I did not leave the house for two weeks. Old bodies take longer to heal and I was no exception. Slowly my bruises faded to yellow.

After the first week, Michi came to remove the stitches and replace the bandage. I asked her about her exams and she said they had gone fairly well but she seemed to have lost some of her enthusiasm for medicine and she admitted she was finding it harder than she had expected.

Michi   I realise how much I've always relied on my mother's knowledge and experience. Everything she did was hands-on healing. I'm not much good at the endless memorising of names and formulae.

Sei   Yet you study so hard and you seem so determined. Don't get discouraged now. Maybe something else is bothering you?

Michi   Dr Kida always gives me hopeless cases to deal with and the patients die. It's not my fault, no one could have saved them, but everyone thinks it is, and I can't help blaming myself.

Sei   I imagine he is quite a demanding teacher.

Michi   He deliberately makes life hard for me. He says I have to be prepared for opposition from the male world of medicine and if he seems to be bullying me it's for my own sake.

Sei   You would think taking you on as a pupil means he sees the need for female doctors.

Michi   He claims he does but he doesn't treat me as an equal. Oh, I shouldn't tell you this but . . . he leans too closely against me when we are examining a patient, or even when I am operating. I am afraid he is going to ask for certain favours in return for his patronage and teaching. People are already gossiping about the amount of time we spend alone together.

Mrs Kida has become cold and spiteful as though she suspects I am already his mistress.

Sei   I wish I could do something to help you.

Michi   I am sorry; I don't know why I am telling you all this. I have no one else to unburden myself to.

Sei   I hope you will always feel you can talk to me.

Michi   You won't tell anyone else, will you?

Of course I promised I would not but that did not prevent me from adding her disclosures to my character study of her. She seemed to me the epitome of the modern woman. Her childhood had been scarred by the civil war; her mother's standing and livelihood were threatened by new legislation; Michi, a young widow, had made the courageous decision to come to Tokyo alone to get the essential qualification. Now I could see that the great city with its bitter conflicts and its fierce competition was crushing her.

I DID NOT SEE Michi again until Satoshi's lecture. We had agreed to go together but on the day she sent me a message to say she would be working late and would meet me there.

The lecture was held in a room in a teahouse called the Azuma, behind Ginza. It was not far but I was still in some pain and would have liked to take a rickshaw. However, I was too conscious of our dwindling funds. Reluctantly I had handed over Keinen's diary to Tae and she had taken it back to the bookseller, Kuruba Gozaemon, but he had denied ever seeing it and there was no record of the sale or of the amount I still owed him. Once she realised that, Tae had not pressed him to return the deposit. She had tried instead to sell the book up and down the street in Kanda but no one wanted it. Some said it was a forgery, others that it was an unfashionable subject and one, the last one, looked at it for a long time and then took off his eyeglasses and in a low voice told her to hide it away or better yet burn it.

All this gave my contrary wife a new respect for the diary and she brought it home, wrapped it up in silk and oiled paper and hid it under the floorboards.

At least I did not have to worry about the debt to Gozaemon but in the meantime I could not work and I had no income and no savings. So I could not afford a rickshaw to the lecture. I walked slowly, with a cane, reflecting on how old I had become since the assault. It was early evening and the streets were still crowded but I felt invisible among the throng of people who brushed against me or stumbled into me as if they truly did not see me.

I was finding it hard to breathe. Halfway along Ginza I stopped to rest for a moment and ahead of me saw Michi come out of the Rakuzendō, an expensive pharmacy that sold salves and ointments from Shanghai and Hong Kong, eau de Cologne, and exotic perfumes from France, as well as the latest medicines and compounds.

I was about to hurry after her so we could walk together but Takayuki followed her out; he must have been talking to someone inside the shop. At the sight of him I shrank back against the wall, my heart thudding painfully. He was wearing his usual traditional clothes and walked in his grave, deliberate manner. He took up all the space around him; no one brushed up against him or failed to notice him. In the bustling crowd with its curious mix of styles and fashions he seemed immutable, a symbol of all that was good and honourable from the past, worthy to be preserved.

Was it really this man who had threatened me and set his thugs on me?

He walked alongside Michi and it seemed an act of greater intimacy than if he had given her his arm or held her hand. The turn of his head, the angle of his shoulder said clearly, *This beautiful woman is mine.*

It filled me with discomfort, fear mingled with jealousy.

They went on together and I followed at a distance until they parted at the corner of a narrow street that led down to the Azuma. Michi stopped to gaze at a roughly drawn poster which advertised the lecture on French history and literature (no mention of politics) and gave directions.

I caught up and stood beside her; she turned and greeted me warmly, asking how I was.

Sei   I saw you coming out of the pharmacy.

Michi   Takayuki goes there quite often. It's a fascinating place. All the clerks wear their hair in long queues as though they were Chinese. Mr Kishida makes them all speak Chinese; they go back and forth to China all the time. Mr Kishida knows more about China than anyone, including the Foreign Minister. Takayuki likes talking to him and hearing the latest information.

Sei   I thought he might be buying you perfume.

Michi   He does that too.

The colour rose in her face a little. She was wearing a very high quality silk crepe kimono, patterned with persimmons and bush clover, and a black silk sash. That and the expensive perfume which floated around her exasperated me, though I found it difficult to explain why.

I stomped away, my cane tapping on the cobbles, feeling like a foolish old man.

Michi made no comment on my irritation but came calmly after me, found us a place in the lecture room, helped me onto a cushion and sat down next to me, attracting quite a few glances. There were not many other women there and none as elegantly dressed as Michi.

It was the first time I had attended a meeting organised by the People's Rights Movement and I studied the crowd with interest. They were younger on the whole than the Black Ocean members and a lot less disciplined. Many seemed to be students, wearing European-style caps; others, older, might have been dock workers or merchant seamen, the self-educated types who travelled the world picking up books and ideas. I recognised a couple of newspaper reporters, along with a handful of *sōshi*, among them Ushiwa Teiji. Ushiwa seemed to have lost part of his ear; the wound was half-healed and he had a fresh black eye.

His wounds made me feel nervous. I hoped there was not going to be fighting here. My eyes scanned the crowd, searching for Takayuki's thugs or anyone else who might be an informer.

Before Satoshi's lecture started, a spokesman, one Takagi Hideki, stood up, announced the recent establishment of a new political party, the Freedom Party, and reminded the gathering of their core beliefs:

1. All men of all nations are born equal. Serve your country and the fellowship of mankind.

2. Be loyal to your comrades and adhere to the values of the future: equality, freedom, justice and participation in government.
3. Resist unnecessary taxation and support farmers.
4. Reform unequal treaties with Western governments.
5. Resist extremist ministers and support progressive ones.
6. Support Korean patriots and modernise Korea.

They sounded both like and unlike those I had heard at the Black Ocean meeting.

Satoshi looked impressive in his well-cut Parisian clothes. He started nervously, his words coming out too rapidly and quietly, but Ushiwa shouted at him to speak up. Satoshi glanced out at the crowd and must have spotted Michi. From then on he seemed to address only her. I was determined to concentrate so I could sound intelligent afterwards, since he was sure to ask how it went, but I became distracted by wondering what it would feel like to be confined by trousers. Wouldn't your private parts feel very constricted? And surely it was rather unhealthy? Did you wear a *fundoshi* or did you have Western underwear? I made a mental note to ask him about it.

When I started listening again he was talking about the French Revolution, almost one hundred years ago now, an explosion of idealism, violence and power struggles that had left lasting scars. There was still no true democracy, but heavy taxation and war. Napoleon had declared himself Emperor (*slight tremor of nervousness round the room*), the people had been seduced by his promise of glory and a generation had been decimated.

Nations went to war, Satoshi said, to win honour and respect but Japan should not be tempted down this path. Our country was in a unique position to sit between the West and Asia as moderator and instructor. Japan must become a model country, a laboratory for democracy and moral principles whose citizens lived in equality and peace. Government must be by the people and for the people (*cheers and some boos*).

It was an elaboration of the ideas he had expressed at my house and my attention wandered again. When it returned from a daydream I could not recall, Satoshi had gone on to speak of the great novelists such as Victor Hugo, who described the wretched lives of the poor and had more influence on social reform than most politicians. Japan had to catch up in literature as well as political and judicial systems, commerce and industry. He urged his audience to read novels as they became available in translation, for it was through novels that we learned about other countries and their people (*nodding of heads and murmurs of assent*).

His closing remarks – that if people were being asked to make sacrifices, die for their country and pay taxes, they had to demand the inalienable rights of all human beings – were greeted with enthusiastic applause. Then Takagi suggested questions from the audience.

Q.   Have you yourself done any translations?

A.   I am working on some. And I have helped Master Akabane adapt some tales by Guy de Maupassant for his form of storytelling, *rakugo*.

I felt a little glow of proprietorial pride, as if Monsieur Guy was my own personal invention as well as an old friend, and I missed most of the next question, which was not really a question but some know-all holding forth about Rousseau and the Social Contract. Takagi finally got him to shut up and Satoshi commented that Rousseau was indeed a great thinker, had recently been translated into Japanese, and everyone should read him too.

Q.   What role does our Imperial Family play in your vision of Japan?
A.   Emperors like Napoleon come and go but it is the people who remain (*profound shock all round*).

Takagi said swiftly that of course Okuda-sensei was only referring to the Western empires. Our own Imperial Family was divine and everlasting. A look of disbelief crossed Satoshi's face and he seemed about to argue further, but Takagi announced the lecture was over.

A buzz rose from the audience as they began to chatter among themselves. Ushiwa rushed up to me, greeting me like a blood brother, eager to relate his latest brawl, this time at Kaba-san, another incident in which peasants with legitimate grievances were crushed by police. I eventually got away from him and moved to the back of the room, where Satoshi and Takagi were still discussing the Emperor question. Michi stood next to them.

Takagi   We cannot criticise the Emperor. Such words are the surest way to get our meetings closed down. Be very careful what you say.

Satoshi   The first thing we must fight for is the right to speak freely and to write freely in our newspapers.

Takagi   That is still a long way off.

Satoshi   It is terrible that we should be intimidated and silenced. Look at what happened to Master Akabane. We should fight strenuously against such treatment.

Takagi   No one wants to get beaten up or imprisoned. We have to walk a fine line.

Satoshi   Governments don't give away rights and freedoms. They have to be won with blood.

Michi made no comment on any of this though she listened carefully, turning her gaze from one speaker's face to the other. Then she said quietly to me that she had to leave, and Satoshi immediately announced he would walk with her.

At first the three of us walked abreast. I remembered the romantic scene I had described to Tae, of the two young lovers in the moonlight, and was looking for an excuse to let them walk on together, but when I slowed my pace Michi slowed down too. Luckily an old acquaintance, coming drunkenly out of a tavern, called my name and I was able to stop and have an incomprehensible chat with him. Michi looked as if she would wait for me but I waved her on.

I followed them eventually, walking abruptly away from my inebriated companion while he was still in full stream. The night was not quite how I had imagined it; there was a cold wind, the sky was overcast, and along the river the willow leaves had turned yellow and were drifting into the water. The tinkling *shamisens* all sounded out of tune, and everything made me feel melancholy.

Satoshi had stopped. I was not close enough to hear what he was saying but I thought he was pleading his case and my heart beat faster, applauding his courage.

Michi listened gravely, then took his hand and held it against her cheek.

Heavens! She has accepted him!

But as I approached I saw she was shaking her head and I heard her utter the words, *I am sorry. That will never be possible.*

Satoshi muttered a brief apology and walked away without looking at Michi again. She and I went home mostly in silence. I, ever inquisitive, tried to find out exactly what Satoshi had said, but she evaded my questions. I thought I read regret in her face for what might have been. I was torn between genuine pity for Satoshi and the hope that one day, when he had got over her, he might be free to become my son-in-law.

21

I HAD DONE NOTHING about arranging divorces for my daughters, and the matter came high on my list of pressing concerns, second only to the need to get hold of some money. I thought I might try writing for the newspapers, though my interview with Kyu had still not appeared and I had not been paid for it. Despite spending all day scribbling in the storeroom, Shigure had not yet finished a second story that she felt able to allow anyone else to read. Teru was the only one of us actually earning any money; she continued to knit day and night until her arms ached, and her shawls sold as soon as she had completed them.

Maybe, I thought, we should all learn how to knit – was anyone ever beaten up for the colour of their wool? Dropped stitches were less dangerous than fallen words.

I decided to consult my one remaining son-in-law, Kat'chan, about the following:

1. The interview
2. The fee for the above
3. Further work of the same sort
4. A loan.

I went to the theatre in the morning and caught Kat'chan on his break. It was the day before the dress rehearsal. The sets were still being built, carpenters rushed around with saws and hammers, painters were putting final touches to the flats and cut-outs, riggers in the rafters were rehearsing the flying in and out of scenery, props were being finished and assembled. It all looked utterly chaotic and I could not imagine the play ever being ready in time.

Kat'chan looked as he usually did in the week before an opening, red-eyed, hair standing on end, dishevelled. We sat in his tiny room while he gulped down rice in gruel, the only thing he was able to digest when under stress. Every few minutes someone came to the door with a question and he shouted a reply.

He seemed as pleased to see me as anyone could be in the circumstances and flicked the morning paper over to me. It had been folded open to show a blurred photo of Kyu which made him look beautiful but evil. The headline read: *Foreign Actor Shines at the Shintomi-za* and underneath was my name. I skimmed quickly through the article.

Sei   I didn't write this!

Kat'chan   No, I didn't either. It's been rewritten.

Sei   Didn't they show it to you?

Kat'chan   I didn't ask them to. I gave your two versions to the paper, and then I went away to Mount Yari and forgot all about it. Something happened up there that I want to talk to you about – after this brute of a play is up and running.

Sei   When does it open?

Kat'chan   Day after tomorrow. Will you come? I've kept a ticket for you.

Sei   Definitely. But what about this article?

Kat'chan   What do you make of it? I keep reading it over and over and I can't decide if it's flattering or derogatory.

Sei   It manages to be both at once. On the surface there is praise and admiration, and underneath there is a kind of surprise and anger that a foreigner, a Korean, should be in a position to win such praise. It gives his Korean name, not his Japanese one.

Kat'chan   Give it to me. They couldn't make him look ugly, though, could they? Do you think it will make people want to see the play?

Sei   Probably. The play sounds intriguing and Kyu is going to attract a lot of attention.

Kat'chan   Just hope it's not the wrong sort. The last thing we need is a bunch of anti-Korean agitators coming along.

Sei   Has Kyu seen it?

Kat'chan   He didn't like the photo but he liked being in the paper. He feels invulnerable at the moment. As well as being on stage in black, he is playing the tiger, which is what he always wanted, and Sakutarō is more besotted than ever. Anyway, even though he can read Japanese, I don't think he quite gets all the nuances.

Sei   It's embarrassing to ask, and I didn't even write the article as it is, but my name is on it . . . was there any payment?

Kat'chan   Yuri told me about your troubles. I was really sorry to hear it. I hope you are recovered?

Sei   I'm fine now, thank you.

Kat'chan   I'll chase up the fee. But you'll be performing again soon, won't you?

Sei   If they lift the ban on me – and if I can come up with some new material. Everyone has such thrilling stories these days. It's hard to compete and I have to start all over again.

Kat'chan   It's all dust and illusion anyway. I must go. I'll see you at the opening. Here, take this.

He pulled out a cash box and took from it some coins, which he pressed on me. They added up to about two yen. I had hoped for a bit more but I took it anyway, thanking my son-in-law and wondering what he wanted to talk to me about and what he meant by 'dust and illusion'. I had no time to ask him. There was a huge crash from the stage and the sound of swearing. Kat'chan leaped to his feet and rushed out. When he didn't reappear, I took myself off and went to walk along the river.

I was uneasy about the unpleasant undertone of the newspaper article. I had no grudge against Koreans and I did not want to lend my name to those who did, but to make a fuss about it now would only draw more attention to the article and to my own foolishness. I should have cared more deeply about what I had written; I should have kept a copy. I had treated the whole thing casually, like the fallen words of my storytelling, which were as light and ephemeral as the autumn willow leaves floating away with the tide, but the newspaper had captured those words and set them in print, so they were no longer what I had written nor meant what I had intended.

I wondered what further distortions would be revealed in the play, *Hideyoshi's Invasion*.

There were high expectations for this play and a certain amount of patriotic fervour; the first performance was packed. I squeezed into my seat in a box shared with four others whom Kat'chan had invited. I did not know any of them, but they chatted to me and each other, and offered me the parched nuts at which they were pecking like hungry birds.

The play was originally to be about Hideyoshi's double invasion of Korea in 1592 and 1598. This was still the background, but, as so often happens when a new play is created, the most interesting character had taken over the plot to an extent that the producers, and even the writers, had not foreseen. Once again entertainment had trumped history, squeezing it into a plausible, flattering and inspiring narrative. The actors naturally did not care about political aims and expediencies. Their main loyalty was to the play and their roles in it. Anything theatrical was embraced; if it did not work on stage, they rejected it.

Now the play was about Hideyoshi's commander Konishi Yukinaga, his rivalry with his fellow general Katō Kiyomasa, his triumphs in Korea, his defeat, after Hideyoshi's death, at the battle of Sekigahara, and his execution on the orders of Tokugawa Ieyasu in the year 1600.

Konishi was a compelling character and I found the play gripping as it explored his early life. His father was a wealthy pharmacist who adored and indulged his precociously gifted son. Reports of military campaigns were Konishi's favourite childhood reading and he grew up to be a master of strategy and a persuasive diplomat, adept at lies and deception. He and his father both became Christians (it was the height of the Jesuits' missionary activity in Japan) and Konishi took the name of Dom Agostinho. His daughter was also a fervent believer and she persuaded her husband, Sō Yoshitoshi, another important military commander, to convert to her father's religion.

There were several powerful scenes before the first interval, the highlight being Hideyoshi's presentation to Konishi of the finest horse in the realm. The horse became a symbol of the invaders. As Kyu had told me, it was played by actors of the traditional horse family and, though he had been scathing about them, I thought they acquitted themselves well. The audience loved them. It was not until I saw Kyu's tiger that I would realise how far they fell short.

Because the Shintomi-za used natural lighting, it was possible to see clearly the reactions of everyone present, on stage and off. The play took place in our midst rather than at a distance. At the second interval I realised Takayuki had joined the audience and was sitting not far from me, a little in front and to the right, apparently on his own. He turned several times to glance around and on one of these occasions our eyes met and he made a slight bow of greeting. I spent the rest of the performance watching him and wondering what I would say if he spoke to me.

The story progressed. There was another powerful scene in which Konishi and Katō argued about who would lead the attack on Seoul. Insults were exchanged and the rivals almost drew their swords on each other before Sō Yoshitoshi intervened to calm them down. The victories in Korea were enumerated. Konishi won the race to Seoul, giving thanks to his god and to the holy Maria.

Katō meanwhile was occupying himself wooing a Korean princess and hunting tigers. If Konishi's horse symbolised the power of the invader, the tiger stood for the brave opposition and the terrible suffering of the defeated. Kyu's tiger made the horse seem just what it was, a clever artifice; he summoned up the essence of the animal, its solitary existence in the forest, its lethal predatory power, how it fought for its life, almost overcoming the Japanese general, and how it died, its spirit slipping away, its body destined to become prized meat for a tyrant, its skin a cloak for Katō.

I watched Takayuki's face, wondering what emotions he was feeling and what I might read of them. The boy who had brought the tiger so magnificently to life had been his protégé, his lover. Did he regret handing him on to Sakutarō (who had the role of his life in Konishi)? Kyu was not only beautiful, he had a supreme talent as well. I thought I could read regret and longing, but maybe it was just my imagination.

As the play wound towards its end, Takayuki leaned forward watching intently. I felt he was waiting for something, not just the climax of the play, and I was seized by the premonition that some greater tragedy was about to unfold. By the time the final scene took place – after the defeat at Sekigahara, Konishi declined to commit suicide because of his Christian beliefs and was executed – I fully expected Sakutarō to be beheaded for real. The chilling sound as the sword apparently hit flesh, the blood that spurted, the head that was presented for Ieyasu's inspection, were completely convincing. Takayuki's eyes glittered, the faintest of smiles on his lips. I had no doubt a murder had taken place and I was looking at its perpetrator.

But the illusion of theatre had done its work; my imagination had run away with me. Sakutarō was resurrected to take his bow to tumultous applause.

Takayuki's jaw clenched in disappointment. He stood abruptly and left without looking at me.

THE AUDIENCE SHOUTED and stamped their feet for a full five minutes and departed with that elated buzz that signifies a hit. The play would probably run for years. I went backstage to congratulate Kat'chan.

His tiny cubbyhole was empty but I could hear his voice giving orders for the preset for the next day's performance. Slowly everything quietened, the actors and stage crew left, and the theatre took on the deepened silence of empty buildings after the throng departs and the clamour dies down. Kat'chan finally appeared looking more exhausted than ever. It was hard to believe that by next morning he would have bounced back to his usual energetic self.

Kat'chan So what's your verdict?

Sei   It's a triumph. The story is moving and the

acting and stagecraft superb. The Christian element is powerful, though to be honest it surprised me. I've never seen it openly presented on stage; didn't the censors object?

Kat'chan   It's all right to portray Christianity now. We are a civilised people who allow freedom of religion, after all!

Sei   And why no mention of Admiral Yi?

Kat'chan   Ah, poor Admiral Yi, the Korean hero. I was sorry when they dropped him. He was in the early drafts but the play was running too long so his scenes were cut. His story was too complicated to explain clearly and it detracted from the dramatic narrative.

Sei   He inflicted crushing defeats on the Japanese navy!

Kat'chan   The producers didn't want to dwell on that. Look, I had no say in it. I have to get the play up and running and prevent disasters. There was nearly one tonight. My blood's still frozen. What do you make of this?

He pushed aside a pile of drop sheets and work clothes and took out a long object rolled up in an old jacket. He unwrapped it.

The blade lay naked, the steel glistening.

Kat'chan   Someone substituted it for the prop sword Kyu hands to Konishi's executioner. It's a very quick change: Sakutarō has to duck his head and fall as the sword hits him. He found it quite hard to get the timing right in rehearsal; he went too soon, which looked ridiculous, or too late and got hit. Tonight he would have been determined not to look like a fool – he was possessed by the role and by Konishi's courage.

He did go a bit late – did you hear the thud? He would have lost his head for real if I hadn't double-checked all the props.

Sei   Who would want to kill Sakutarō?

Kat'chan   Well, I can think of quite a few. His fans might adore him but he's upset plenty of people in the company. But what if he wasn't really the target – what if someone wanted the blame to fall on Kyu? Because he's Korean, which everyone knows now from the article? He's responsible for the sword, along with all the other props that relate to Sakutarō's role.

Sei   You don't think Kyu substituted the sword himself?

Kat'chan   Why would he do that? Sakutarō is his protector and Kyu is mad about theatre.

Sei   Maybe someone persuaded him or blackmailed him.

I studied the sword more carefully. I was no expert and really could not tell one blade from another but it looked just like Takayuki's sword, which I had last seen being offered to the Emperor in the Black Ocean meeting. I remembered Takayuki's intense anticipation before the play's final scene. He had known the sword was there. Had he even placed it there himself? I thought I had seen regret on his face when he watched Kyu on stage, but maybe it had been a perverted sorrow at the sacrifice of someone who had loved him, as a man might regret plucking a beautiful flower only to crush it.

Sei   Could someone have put the sword there without you seeing it?

Kat'chan   It's quite possible. I can't be everywhere at once, and it's often chaotic backstage, as you know.

Sei   You should go to the police.

Kat'chan   Now? After a successful opening night? There's no way I'm going to the police. I'll pretend it never happened. I thought you could take the sword home and hide it. There's nowhere safe to put it here.

I really did not want to have anything to do with Takayuki or his sword but I could not very well refuse my son-in-law who had been so good to me. I followed him to the props room, where he found a scabbard for the sword, rolled it up again in its jacket and put it in a big canvas bag. While he did this I looked around with considerable curiosity. The horse and the tiger rested on racks, their skins empty, their heads held upright, their eyes bright. They still had some unsettling vestiges of animal life. I ran my fingers over the skins – they were from real animals, and smelled faintly of camphor. The tiger's fur felt not unlike Aka's; its markings were even more astonishing close-up. I thought of the tiger Kyu had described in the shadows of the forest.

The horse's tail was long and silky like the hair of a woman. The heads were skilfully carved and painted, with glass eyes, wooden teeth and fleshy looking tongues. I wondered at the living creatures that had been mastered and killed by men only to be recreated by them in the fantasy that was theatre. I wondered what narratives lay beneath the skin. I wished the tiger could talk and tell me its tale.

Kat'chan   You know there are meant to be ghosts in all theatres? I've never seen one but apparently they're here – old actors who can't leave, stagehands who died in accidents.

Sei   Maybe one of them swapped the swords.

Kat'chan   Don't joke about it. There are moments when the play seems to transcend itself and some almost sacred state takes over both players and audience. That's when the theatre's at its most dangerous, when accidents happen. They say the dead are jealous of the living – they are warning them not to come too close.

Now it was my blood that chilled as we left the empty theatre and walked towards my house. Dusk was falling and lights were coming on in the streets and shops. There was a smell of roasting chestnuts. It all seemed so ordinary, while my mind was still reeling from the play and from Kat'chan's revelation. I thought everyone would notice that we walked through the streets carrying the sword of a ruthless man. Was he even now following us? Would he appear at any moment and demand it back?

Kat'chan   I saw something on Mount Yari.

Sei   Is that what you wanted to tell me?

Kat'chan   Mmm. I don't know if it was a ghost, or an angel, or my own soul. It was like a great shadow that walked with me on the opposite peak. It waved back at me when I waved and there were circles like rainbows round its head.

Sei   Many people have visions in the mountains. That is why there are shrines on peaks and so many pilgrims.

Kat'chan   I've never had one before and I've never considered myself a pilgrim. I'm not at all a mystical person. I'm an alpinist. But I can't stop thinking about it. Was it a sign? What was it telling me? The play got me thinking about Christianity. I've been to church a couple of times. God does speak to individuals. He sends angels to them. Was he sending me an angel? I feel I've been called to do something special, but I don't know what. Leave the theatre? Join a church?

Sei   But you love the theatre! You've devoted your life to it. You wouldn't think of leaving it?

Kat'chan   I used to love it. But now I see it for what it is.

Sei   Dust and illusion?

Kat'chan   Exactly.

Sei   Well, everything's that. Isn't that what Buddhism preaches too? This world of dew and so on and so on? Why Christianity? Why not Buddhism? Plenty of visions and angels there!

Kat'chan   I feel as if I'm being called by Christianity.

Sei   Have you talked to Yuri about it?

Kat'chan   There never seems to be time. You're the first person I've told apart from the pastor.

The word pastor upset me. I had a vague feeling Christian priests were unmarried. I did not want to lose the one son-in-law left to me. Christianity was still something strange and exotic. During the Tokugawa years it had been banned under pain of death, and even though there was now freedom of religion and many modern thinkers were extolling Christianity as an essential part of being civilised, to ordinary people it still seemed a little suspect, a little dangerous. There was no doubt that this added to the success of the play I had just seen; Konishi Yukinaga's Christian journey was a gripping narrative, but I wanted that story to stay on stage, not jump out, capture my son-in-law and take him away from me.

We came to my house. Aka, who considered Kat'chan part of the family, leaped up with an excited yelp. Kat'chan patted him absent mindedly, his face drawn. I told him he was overtired, he should go home and try to sleep. He handed the sword to me and we said goodnight.

Everyone was home, Tae preparing dinner, Teru knitting, Shigure scribbling. Of course they all wanted to know what I was carrying. I said it was some mountaineering equipment Kat'chan had asked me to store for him and I put it away at the back of the cupboard where we kept the futons. I tried to distract them by relating the play scene by scene, describing the sets and the costumes, the props and special effects, the actors, the horse and Kyu's extraordinary performance as the tiger, but when Tae went in to prepare the beds she found the bundle and in her usual inquisitive way unwrapped it. I heard her gasp and hurried in.

Tae	It's just a stage prop, isn't it?
Sei	The scabbard is. Inside is the real thing.

Tae drew the sword out and we both stared at it just as Kat'chan and I had earlier. There was something horribly compelling about its long curved blade, dark and gleaming.

Tae	It looks like an old one.
Sei	There's probably a maker's name on it somewhere.

I don't want to look at it too closely. It's like a snake. I feel it might rear up and strike me.

Tae   What's it doing here?

Sei   Somebody replaced a prop with it. Kat'chan found it in time to prevent a murder on stage. He asked me to hide it.

Tae   Do you think we could pawn it? It must be worth a fortune.

Sei   We really don't want to draw attention to it.

Tae   But who does it belong to? Who planted it? Shouldn't Kat'chan go to the police?

Sei   We should just hide it and forget about it for now.

Tae   It's not going to fit under the floorboards with the book. And we can't leave it in the cupboard. The girls might find it.

Sei   I'll wrap it in a bamboo blind and put it in the rafters.

We put it back in the cupboard for the time being and went to bed.

I HID THE SWORD in the roof over the kitchen but I could not forget it. It had the same effect on me as Keinen's diary – as if I'd put a pot of embers up there that at any moment was going to burst into flames and burn the house down. I tried to work on my long story about the former samurai, the French teacher, and the young woman whom they both love who wants to be a doctor, but Takayuki's actions had brought it to a halt. I found his character a challenge, to say the least. Could he really have planned the death on stage of a famous and much-loved actor, implicating his former lover? Like the assault on me, it seemed completely out of character with the honourable, chivalrous image he presented to the world. He was too complex for my simple form of storytelling, which required heroes and villains but not a mixture of the two. Yet he continued to intrigue me; he behaved as if the rest of the world belonged to him and he could treat it as he liked. Was it the result or the cause of the strange deference he commanded? Would he ever solve that mystery? Would I?

Tae kept asking awkward questions, which did not help with the story's progress.

A few days later, needing a distraction, I went next door to Hirano's place. I wanted to talk to Satoshi. Chie, her lip curling in annoyance as she spoke, told me he was with her husband and Ushiwa Teiji, having one of their politico–literary debates. I made my way to the detached room where Hirano held sway. It was early evening, a couple of days before the October full moon; the air was frosty and moonlight gleamed on the stone lantern and the little pond.

They had already started drinking. The screens were all open. Hirano did not seem to feel the cold. His usual fishy smell floated around him and his limbs spread out from his vast mass; I counted them just to check he did not have eight. His domed skull gleamed with sweat and his eyes twinkled maliciously under his heavy lids. I sat as close to the brazier as possible, shivery as I always seemed to be lately.

Ushiwa   Master! Greetings! Have you been fighting for the cause lately?

Sei   Trying hard to avoid it! How about you?

Ushiwa   I'm off next week to Chichibu. That's going to be a big one. Now the Freedom Party has been formed we have a real alliance – activists, intellectuals, workers, farmers. We're really going to take on the government. Satoshi's coming, aren't you?

Satoshi   Well, I don't know. I can't just leave my pupils.

Hirano   Chichibu's your homeland, isn't it? Your family must be suffering like everyone else.

Satoshi   I haven't seen them since I left for France.

Hirano   That's shockingly unfilial. It's high time you went back. And get your parents to find you a wife while you're there. A treasure like mine!

Ushiwa   There won't be time for matchmaking. We're going to join the Army of the Poor and demand justice from the government. And teach a few of those inhuman grasping moneylenders a lesson while we're about it. Anyway, Satoshi's got his eye on a young lady not so far from here.

Hirano   And who might that be?

Ushiwa   Satoshi, you're the silk expert. Did you see what she was wearing to your lecture? That kimono must have cost a packet!

Satoshi   I noticed.

Hirano   You mean the doctor? Steer clear of her – she's involved with Yamagishi Takayuki, the samurai fellow who comes round here so often. My wife thinks the world of him but he's an informer for the Ministry of the Interior. The Korean boy is one of his spies and so is the doctor woman. If she came to your lecture it was so she could report back to him.

Ushiwa   He thought she came because she fancied him! In her best kimono and all – paid for by her lover, no doubt.

Satoshi   I thought she was interested in what I had to say.

Hirano   Just pretending. Yamagishi has her completely under his control – which makes my wife insanely jealous. She'd spread her legs for him in an eye blink, even though she's old enough to be his mother. I keep telling her, why would he be interested in an old bag like you when he's got a young woman infatuated with him?

Ushiwa   Not to mention the young man!

Hirano   He's been handed on, I hear, to the great Sakutarō. But Yamagishi still has his talons in him.

At that moment Chie came along the verandah, her expression furious. She knelt silently at the door and slipped a tray inside. An indescribably delicious smell arose from three dishes of oysters, the first of the season, and one of abalone, stewing in their shells. She also delivered another two flasks of warmed sake; she left without saying a word.

Hirano   I suppose one day she'll poison me but meanwhile . . . *kampai!*

Ushiwa   They're surviving on millet and gruel in Chichibu. Spare a thought for the suffering poor. *Kampai!*

Satoshi did not eat or drink any more. He sat staring miserably into space, probably imagining all that Michi might have told Takayuki – his poetry, his proposal – no doubt hearing their mocking laughter. I wanted to distract him somehow.

Sei   I wondered if we might try some more of Monsieur Guy's stories.

Satoshi   I won't have time for a while. I've decided – I will go to Chichibu with Ushiwa. It's time I went home.

I protested that he should not go, he should think of his work and his future and avoid any sort of violent confrontation that might land him in prison, but Hirano's words had made him determined to leave Tokyo and it was hard to argue that he should not visit his family. He had talked about them during our summer writing sessions and I knew they were struggling, like all silk producers and farmers. They had borrowed money to expand while business was booming and rates were low but the collapse of the silk market in Europe and the severe economic policies of the current Finance Minister had reduced their income and pushed interest rates up.

Satoshi's oldest sister wrote frequently, begging him to come home. His parents were ageing, the second sister had left home to work at a spinning factory in Osaka, and the younger brother was running wild.

He and Ushiwa departed two days later, getting a ride on a supply train on the new railway line that was thrusting northwards. He told me he intended to come back in a few weeks. He left his books and his other belongings in his room and had paid his rent until the end of the year. I went to Ueno station to see them off – they seemed a symbol of our nation, pushing forwards, taking off into the unknown, even though the tracks to their destination were still to be laid.

While I was at Ueno it occurred to me I might take the train out to Yokohama and visit Shigure's husband, Ono Renzō. I had to do something about getting my daughters out of the house. I was very fond of them but I was finding it impossible to concentrate on my work while they were around. They needed to go off and live their own lives. They could not stay at home forever, but if they were to remarry, first they had to be divorced.

Renzō was at work in his smart new office, recently erected between the merchants' godowns and the tiny Chinese food shops of the port. He was too busy to see me immediately, sent his regrets via his secretary and asked me to come back at midday. I wandered around for a while, looking at the foreign ships, steamers and clippers, and admiring the Western-style bungalows on the Bluff, their large gardens now bare and flowerless apart from a few scarlet maples. Women walked past wearing wide dresses and fur stoles, often carrying little lapdogs. Secretly I had always wanted one of those tiny dogs; I wondered if Tae would ever let a dog in the house. I didn't think it was likely. Anyway, Aka would probably eat it.

The church clock struck midday and I went back to the office. Renzō came out, greeted me rather perfunctorily and led me down an alley to a very expensive restaurant hidden behind the godowns. He was greeted fervently – he didn't need to tell me that he had become an important person in the district, but he did, spending the first half hour of the meal describing his latest deals and developments and how much money he was making. Last time I saw him he had been deflated and miserable. Now confidence had restored his good looks. So many people were struggling in this new world of ours but he was flourishing. He was sharp and hard-headed and did not cling to outmoded practices of the past – except, when we finally got around to the purpose of my visit, when it came to marriage.

Renzō   I hope you've come to tell me Shigure is coming home. I have arranged it all. I've hired a housekeeper. I've set aside a room for her work. I've calculated she will have at least four hours a day to herself, time when she can do her writing. I'm not averse to her having a hobby. I consider myself a modern man. As a matter of fact, I am quite proud of her. Once she has children she may find her ideas change but maybe she could write little tales for young people. That would be charming.

Sei   All of this is very good of you, and I'll tell her what you are prepared to do, but I must warn you – well, I came to ask you for a divorce.

Renzō   I've thought about it a lot since I saw you. Her story showed me that it's me she really loves. I want her back and I will wait for her. I don't care about the other man. By the way, has she recovered from pneumonia?

Sei   She never had pneumonia and there is no other man! That was just in the story.

Renzō   My parents were worried it might be consumption. They are trying to persuade me to divorce her too. But I won't. I'll wait for her forever.

Nothing I said could make him change his mind. As I left he asked if I needed any money. I was extremely tempted to borrow from him, as I'd hoped to at the beginning of the summer, but it seemed too much like signing a contract to return Shigure to him. I said untruthfully and with great regret that everything was fine.

Renzō   I heard you were banned from performing.

Sei   Just a little misunderstanding. I'll be back on stage in no time.

Renzō   Well, let me know. Business is going well and I can always afford to help you out. You will always be my father-in-law.

I returned to Tokyo feeling I had accomplished nothing and frustrated by an offer of money that I could not accept. When I related the events and the offer to Tae, she did not speak for a full minute and then she ran into my study where Shigure was reading and slapped her.

Shigure   What was that for? What have I done now?

Tae   You must go back to your husband. Your father's going to tell you what he is prepared to do for you, the sacrifices he is making. You don't know your luck. There's not one man in a thousand who would treat you as he wants to. You cannot stay here any longer.

Shigure started weeping and swearing she would sooner throw herself in the river, that she could not write in a cage and she hated Renzō. She would never, ever go back, and there followed a screaming match that brought all the neighbours out into the street to listen.

As I said before, Shigure had a will like steel and not even her mother's rage could make her budge. Determined as Tae was, she was several inches shorter than Shigure and not strong enough to throw her out physically, though she tried. Eventually Teru and I calmed them down and imposed a kind of peace but they did not address each other directly for days and could hardly bear to be in the same room. Tae and Teru ganged up against me, blaming me for bringing Shigure up too leniently and spoiling her, and for passing on to her the fatal talent and desire for storytelling.

AGAIN THE ATMOSPHERE in the house became unbearable. It looked as though Shigure would be staying at home forever, so even though my meeting with one son-in-law had not gone very well, I decided to go and see another one, Teru's estranged husband, Tensa, who was having a very successful run at a *yose* hall, the Aosora, in Kanda. I suggested to Shigure that she might like to come with me. Tae tried to forbid her from leaving the house; Shigure naturally decided she would go, and she set about getting ready. She had become quite slovenly during her months of being a writer and I had forgotten how attractive she could look when she made an effort.

I noticed as we walked through the streets how men's eyes appraised her willow-like slenderness and her pale well-shaped face, which for us at home was usually marred by a scowl but today held a calm and pleasant expression.

Shigure   I've been in the house too long. I'd forgotten how wonderful all this is. This is what I want to write about, Father, this huge city and its people. If only I could capture it!

Sei   Each one with a tale to tell – though most of those tales are extraordinarily dull.

Shigure   I can make even the dullest enthralling.

Sei   Well, we all long to read something else from you.

Shigure   You can't rush a story, Father, you know that.

I was familiar with that excuse but I reflected how much easier it was for a person supported by her parents and without children to use it. I did not utter these thoughts. I didn't really think my daughter would throw herself in the river as she had threatened, but I was not going to take that risk.

Tensa's hall was packed and we had trouble finding a space but some people moved up for us and we managed to squeeze in on the end of a row. Tensa told old stories – the *tanuki*, or racoon dog, who turns into a cooking pot, the God of Death and the fake doctor, the fisherman's wife who reforms her layabout husband, the haircut, how to eat soba – the tales of human foolishness, greed, compassion and redemption that have been told and retold for hundreds of years. He gave each one his own special treatment, though, with puns and double meanings that came so rapidly the audience tried to stifle their laughter so as not to miss the next one. Yūdai emphasised these with the music, switching from *shamisen* to flute to drum, his expression also a counterpoint to the jokes. He was a good-looking young man and there was an unmistakable erotic tension between him and Tensa which added to the thrill.

People came four or five times, the man sitting next to me told me in the interval, until they could recite the stories with the jokes word for word.

Jack Green was also in the audience. I had not seen him as he was sitting behind us, but in the interval he came and knelt beside Shigure and we all chatted about nothing in particular until the clappers sounded for the second half and he returned to his place at the back.

Shigure sighed. I whispered to her that she would breathe away all her happiness, as we used to tell the girls when they were children, but I did not assign any special meaning to that sigh.

The second half was taken up with one long, ribald, outrageous and poignant story about the efforts of a woman to regain the affections of a husband who does not seem to love her anymore. While praying to the goddess Kannon about her problems, she is granted the power to take on various different forms – a geisha, a youth, a samurai warrior, a young monk, even a cat. The husband falls in love with every one of them, realising in the end that they are all his wife. Tensa made each role so charming, so seductive, he had the audience completely in love with him by the time he ended with the traditional words: *And now I leave you in the capable hands of the next story.*

I was left with the usual mix of emotions: elation at his success, admiration for the continuing power of storytelling, and envy of his energy and daring, of his youth. When I thought of my poor daughter, Teru, at home, crying herself blind, knitting until her arms fell off, I felt sad and angry. I did not want to talk to Tensa in this mood, so Shigure and I left him to his adoring fans and walked home.

Shigure   You know, Father, I think that story was about Tensa and Teru.
Sei   And your story wasn't about you and Renzō?
Shigure   In a way it was, but not in the way Renzō thought. We make up what we wish people would be, not what they are. Maybe Tensa would love his wife if she had a bit more fantasy in her life.
Sei   You mean she should dress up as a cat?
Shigure   She could try dressing up as a boy!

Once she got an idea in her head, Shigure could not relinquish it. She hurried off home to tell Teru while I thought I would avoid another family clash and have a peaceful smoke in a teahouse. I was puffing away happily when from the back of the room I heard someone who must have been at the performance talking about Tensa. I picked out the usual praise and then his companion said something derogatory about *okama*. My ears pricked up, sensitive as I was to the changing attitudes towards *nanshoku*, and to anything that concerned one of my sons-in-law, but I could not eavesdrop further as Jack Green appeared next to me and asked if he could join me.

I would have preferred my own company but of course could not refuse someone to whom I was so indebted. Then I had to put up with his effusive praise of Tensa's performance.

Jack   And you, Master, when will we see you back again?

Sei   I am working on something new. I hope my ban will be lifted before the end of the year.

Jack   I wanted to tell you about a new invention. Have you heard of shorthand?

Sei   I have not.

Jack   It's a rapid writing system that has just been perfected for the Japanese language. A stenographer records your performance word for word; then it can be written up and printed. You know how hard it is to capture on paper the words that sound so fine when we speak them. Now we can be instant novelists: serialisation in newspapers, then book publication. I am going to have my next presentation taken down in this way. You should try it too.

Sei   If I ever get something finished and am allowed to perform, I will.

Jack   I wonder if we should join forces and help each other out in some way. It's embarrassing to mention it, but if you are ever in any need, please don't hesitate to ask.

Sei   That's very generous of you.

I should have been more grateful but in fact it was rather humiliating to be offered assistance by my younger foreign rival. I called for the waitress to bring me another pipe and smoked for a while in silence.

Jack   Your daughter looked very well.

Sei   Surprisingly well, given the headaches she is causing us.

Jack   May I ask, is she married? I know she is living at home.

Sei She is neither married nor unmarried. She's left her husband and wants to divorce him. He wants her back. She and her mother fight about it all day long.

Jack The truth is, Master, I like her. I like her very much. It's too much to hope for but when her affairs are settled, would you consider me as a son-in-law?

Sei Nothing would give me greater pleasure, but I am afraid Shigure does not want to be married to anyone. Please don't build up your hopes. She is quite determined to be alone so she can write.

Jack She is so wonderful!

Sei Don't waste your time yearning after her. She is very wilful and she would break your heart. Besides, it is my wife's opinion that if she is to be married to anyone, she should go back to her husband.

Jack Not if he makes her unhappy.

Sei It's not a good idea to have two writers in one family, you know. Who will pay the rent on time, order the charcoal and do the washing? Who will look after the children if they come? Think of the children – will they be English or Japanese? And consider your family. We must be realistic. If they disapprove of you performing on stage they will be horrified if you marry a Japanese woman, one who has been divorced. It is not the same as taking a geisha as a mistress; that happens all the time and is easy to overlook. Marriage is a public statement, an alliance between families.

Jack looked glum and said he was ready to cut his ties with his family and ally himself with a new one but the more I thought about it the more preposterous the idea seemed. I told him to forget the whole thing. My pipe had gone out, and though the teahouse owner offered me another one, I decided it was time to go home.

I kept his proposals of marriage, collaboration and money to myself for the time being. What had lodged in my mind most strongly was the shorthand suggestion. I could not get over what a brilliant idea it was. Of course in ancient times scholars and students used a kind of shorthand which evolved into the *katakana* form of writing but I suspected often even they could not work out what they had written and the symbols were more a jog to the memory than a full record. To be able to declaim with all the inventiveness and improvisation that arose during performance and have that taken down – it gave me much-needed inspiration to press on with my story.

To my surprise, Teru took to Shigure's plan enthusiastically, and for the next couple of days they shut themselves up with some old clothes they had bought from the pawnbroker, giggling a lot.

Then Teru announced she was going back to her husband and asked me to go with her.

She was dressed in her usual clothes; they were quite plain but as always she managed to look stylish with a crisp white collar at her neck and one of her colourful shawls round her shoulders. I teased her about having no tail or whiskers but she patted the bundle she and Shigure had prepared and told me it was all in there.

It was one of Tensa's rest days and he and Yūdai were at home. Yūdai was practising music and Tensa was sitting by the hearth, eating an orange. His mother gave a cry of delight at seeing Teru, whipped off her apron, thrust it at Teru and sank down next to her son as though she had just been rescued from some natural disaster. In fact, when I looked round the house, it did look as if it had suffered a catastrophe. Obviously the old lady had found caring for her two bachelors beyond her.

Teru tied back her sleeves and got to work. I sat for a while with Tensa and we shared another orange. I told him how much I had enjoyed his show and congratulated him.

Tensa   It was very good of you to attend. I'm afraid my work is very poor but it seems to please the crowd. I'm glad your daughter has come back. We've missed her.

Sei   I hope things will work out now.

Tensa   I will do my best.

He didn't seem too happy at the prospect and cast a desperate kind of 'help me' look at Yūdai but the musician was watching Teru scouring dishes and singing quietly to herself and did not meet his eye.

I said goodbye to my daughter and walked home, hoping she had done the right thing. Remembering my conversation with Tensa in the summer, I was afraid she was exposing herself to more disappointment; he had made it clear he was not attracted to women. I did not think a little play-acting was going to change that. But if rumours about his sexual preferences were circulating, the sooner he could get Teru pregnant the better.

M Y WIFE WAS talking to Chie outside the lodging house. Chie was holding the morning paper. They both turned and beckoned to me.

Tae   There's been a riot in Chichibu. Thousands of protesters have attacked town offices and moneylenders' houses and burned the records of their taxes and debts. They're still fighting – the government dispatched troops.

Chie   And poor Mr Okuda went there to see his family. My husband and Ushiwa Teiji persuaded him. If anything's happened to him, I'll never forgive them.

Sei   Ushiwa went with him. They travelled together.

Chie   If there's any fighting, he'll be in the thick of it. He's probably persuaded Mr Okuda to join in, armed with a bamboo spear or something equally useless.

Sei   Give me the paper.

I read the article a couple of times, trying to squeeze the last drop of information from it. It said very little, just reported the disturbance and concluded the rioters would soon be dealt with by the police and a crack army unit which had been sent by train from Tokyo to Ōmiya.

Ōmiya used to be considered remote and inaccessible, nestled in the mountains north of Tokyo. I suddenly realised how the railroad was shrinking our country, how small the world was becoming. The telegraph was doing the same thing; the rioters, it seemed, had not bargained for the news of their attacks reaching Tokyo almost immediately over the new wires whose poles sprouted like a single line white forest alongside the railway tracks.

News trickled in slowly over the next few days. At first the authorities tried to present the disturbance as one more peasant riot, but after a few enterprising journalists made their way to Chichibu to gather eyewitness accounts in the modern fashion, it became clear that this was far more than local unrest. The self-styled Army of the Poor numbered around ten thousand men, who were well organised and well armed, though they lacked the modern weapons of the government troops. Their grievances were genuine and their alliance with members of the new Freedom Party turned their struggle for justice into something wider: a challenge to the current system and a demand to have a say in it – that is, almost a civil war.

Articles were censored and newspapers shut down. In less than two weeks the Army of the Poor fell apart and its leaders took to the mountains. Most were hunted down, killed or captured. By the end of the first week of November it was all over.

No news came of Satoshi; he became first in my list of anxieties that woke me in the early hours of the morning. I found myself praying for him and unravelling the threads of fate that had drawn him to Chichibu: his concern for his family, Ushiwa's encouragement, his disillusionment with Michi. I recalled in those hours of darkness and increasing winter cold the hot summer days when we had discussed Monsieur Guy and wondered if I would ever have such pleasure again.

One evening in mid-November, Michi called at our house on the way home from the clinic. It had turned very cold and I suggested she should join us round the hearth but she said she had to speak to me in private, so I took her into my study and closed the door. We were trying to economise on fuel so there was no brazier; our breath hung in the air as we spoke and my fingers and toes gradually went numb.

Michi   Satoshi was arrested. His trial is in two weeks. He's in Kosuge prison.

Sei   How do you know?

Michi   Takayuki found out. He has contacts in the Ministry of the Interior. I made a terrible mistake a little while ago. I told him about the lecture. He wanted to know every detail, who was there, what Satoshi said. I'm afraid I reported his comment about emperors. And then, I don't know why, I told him Satoshi had asked me to marry him. I think I was trying to make him laugh and forget about politics but I only succeeded in enraging him. Now I am afraid he will use his contacts to demand a long jail sentence or even death.

Sei   If anyone can persuade him to be merciful it is you.

Michi   I've tried everything. I've promised I will do anything he wants. If only you knew, Master, how that proposal has tormented me. If only I could have accepted it. I fell in love with Satoshi when he spoke the words of that poem. I have dreamed about us being together and all we could do to create a better world. He would bring out the best in me, while Takayuki brings out the worst. But now I have betrayed him and Takayuki will never let me go.

Her words brought tears to my eyes, foolish, sentimental old man that I was, but she did not weep. Her beautiful face remained undistorted by emotion. Only her fingers betrayed her feelings, clenching and unclenching in her lap.

Michi   I thought you should know. You and Satoshi were good friends and he admired you greatly. You may be able to contact him in prison, write to him or visit him.

Sei   I will do all I can, I promise.

Michi   My father was executed by mistake because he was in the wrong place at the wrong time. I couldn't bear that to happen to Satoshi as well.

Sei   Let's pray it won't come to that. Is Ushiwa Teiji in prison with him?

Michi   I don't know what happened to Ushiwa. I doubt he will come out of it alive.

I thought I would try and visit Satoshi, though I had never been to a prison and did not know what was allowed. I imagined that in Satoshi's position I would most want food, tobacco and something to write with. Tae, Shigure and I set about arranging practical gifts: dried persimmons, parched nuts, paper and ink. Every day was colder. We had little spare money to buy what we needed, so I walked over to Kanda to see if I could borrow from Tensa. He was out but my daughter Teru welcomed me and made me come in and have tea.

I scrutinised her face. She had changed in some way; the drawn, sad look had gone, replaced by a merry expression; she had even put on a little weight, which suited her. When I told her my errand, she immediately went to a small desk and took a box out of one of its drawers.

Teru   Poor Satoshi! Of course we must help him. Let's do it while Mother is asleep. She already thinks I'm robbing my husband.

Sei   I hope she's treating you well.

Teru   I threaten to go home if she tries to bully me. That usually shuts her up. I've taken over the finances – my husband and Yūdai are useless at that side of things. They are doing well at the moment but it doesn't occur to them to save. I am putting a little away each month. When I have enough, I'll invest it somewhere, maybe in property, like Renzō. I'd like to have a little shop where I can sell my knitting directly. Speaking of knitting, I made a muffler and gloves for you for the winter. You can give them to Satoshi and I'll make you another set.

Sei   That's very kind of you. You look happy. How's everything going?

Teru   Everything's going very well. Not quite as I expected but . . . Father, it's embarrassing to talk with you. Let's just say I am happy for now.

And that was all she would say. My curiosity was piqued and I tried to find out more but there was only so much I could discuss with my daughter without unseemly prying.

The old lady woke up and called for Teru to take her to the privy. She seemed to have deteriorated since my previous visit – she did not know who I was – but even caring for her did not dent Teru's cheerfulness.

Tensa must have really made an effort, I thought as I went home.

Teru gave me three yen. I spent one on buying Satoshi's gifts and kept two in case I had to bribe the guards.

KOSUGE WAS ONE of the new prisons built in the Western style and supposedly run on Western principles of humane punishment but even these new prisons could not adequately cope with the thousands arrested in those years of riots and uprisings. The concepts of long-term imprisonment and prison labour were quite new and I had not really grasped what they meant until I went to Kosuge.

It was located north-west of Tokyo, in Yamanashi prefecture, and it took me all day to get there. I had to take a rickshaw I really could not afford to a post station on the outskirts of Tokyo and then hire a horse and boy for the rest of the way. The boy was not talkative so I learned nothing from him save that many people lately had been making this journey, seeking news of their sons and brothers, husbands, fathers and friends.

I arrived too late to go to the prison so I found shelter for the night in a run-down lodging house and prepared myself to face its bad food followed by its fleas and bedbugs. It reminded me of the places I had stayed in as a young man when I toured both Kansai and Kantō, telling stories and gathering new ones.

The lodging house was owned by a woman with poorly dyed hair and, I thought, a grasping nature, hidden under a false manner of kindness and concern. I tried to haggle over the price but she would not take less than fifty sen, saying it was the last bed she had left, and there were others she had promised it to, but I was an old man who had come a long way and aroused her pity and so on and so on. She wore a stained kimono with a grubby frayed collar, was voluble and gave herself airs, using words that were not quite right – *composure* when she meant *compassion*, *solitude* when she meant *solidarity*. Tired as I was, I became fascinated by her as a character. I could picture her as the greedy woman in the folktale, 'The Little Sparrow', who threw stones at sparrows to break their legs so she could then demonstrate her kindness in the hope of their reward. It was a story I had told many times and now I wondered if I might not revive it.

The evening meal was served in a small, smoky room which smelled of stale cooking oil and past meals. There was a space in the corner near an old man which I slipped into, immediately regretting it, for the odour that came from him was even more unpleasant than that of the room, the sad smell of the old, mostly urine. No wonder everyone else had avoided him. I greeted him and told him my name and, when he made no response, concluded he was probably senile. I wondered why he was there: maybe he was some elderly relative whom Madame Composure was obliged to look after.

Since the meal was as bad as I expected, the rice sour and fizzy on the tongue, the vegetables overcooked, I did not eat much, just drank the stewed, bitter tea.

The old man leaned towards me and said, 'Once there was a lord's castle on the hill behind the prison. Abe Tokumasa held out for ten weeks against the Uesugi but they defeated him in the end, made him watch his sons disembowel themselves and then took his head before burning the castle with the survivors inside.'

'Grandpa's away!' someone commented loudly from the end of the room. 'Don't encourage him, sir. He'll wear your ears out with his fantasies.'

'The ghosts are still there,' the old man went on, not heeding the interruption. 'They walk through the prison at night but they are the only ones who can pass freely through those walls.'

His breath stank of decay but I did not move away. I thought with a flicker of excitement that he might be one of those old people you sometimes met in remote villages who were a storehouse of ancient tales and legends that had never been written down.

'His youngest daughter was hidden by her nurse and lived. She grew up not knowing she was from the Abe family. She was a kind and clever girl and she married the son of the village headman. Then came a terrible famine when no one had any food, and this girl went into the mountains to look for wild taro. She lost her way and, as night fell, stumbled upon a beautiful mansion she had never seen before. There was no one inside but the kettle was boiling over the hearth and food had been prepared. She slept beneath a quilt of silk. In the morning, breakfast appeared on a tray beside her bed, and the kettle was still boiling. The house was full of treasures but she took nothing, just an old basket from the verandah to carry home the few taro roots she had found. When she left, she bowed deeply and thanked the mysterious house. As she went home, the basket became heavier and heavier until she could hardly lift it, and from that day on, no matter how much taro they took from the basket, it never emptied. That's why that family became so successful and their daughters married samurai.'

He glanced at me to see the effect the story had had on me and when I smiled and nodded he went on – stories about fox spirits and ghosts, mountain men who kidnapped young women and ate their children, mysterious voices, apparitions that warned of illness and death, legless horses, enchanted snakes.

Everyone else had gone to bed and the lamps were almost out. The landlady appeared and led the old man away. She apologised to me and spoke gently to him but I could see she was pinching his arm and when they were beyond the door he gave a cry of pain. I was sure she had kicked him.

She came back to show me to the room I was sharing with four or five others, but before she left me she whispered, 'If you have any gifts for a prisoner, give them to me. My husband works in the prison; he will make sure they get to the right person. We don't want any renovation, we do it out of pure charisma. Those poor wretches!'

Really, she sounded almost poetic, but I did not want to entrust Satoshi's bundle to her. I lay awake for a long time, the old man's stories and the woman's lies and fabrications going through my mind while the fleas had a feast.

In the morning, one of my companions of the previous night advised me quietly not to give her anything, as neither she nor her husband ever passed gifts on to prisoners but kept them for themselves. I asked if I should go through the officials; he replied that they too would probably steal anything of value and I would have to bribe them anyway.

Still, having got that far, I was not going to leave without trying.

The prison was built on the site of a brickworks and it was now the prisoners who made the red bricks that were such a feature of modern architecture and a symbol of our new world. I had not known that before, and since then I have not felt comfortable walking down Ginza. There were many people like me trying to get information and it took me a long time to reach an official, who could do no more but confirm that Satoshi was indeed held there. He could not take my parcel. Visitors were out of the question. I asked about Ushiwa, offering one of my yen coins, and after a prolonged search through the lists, he said coldly without looking at me that Ushiwa Teiji had died of wounds in prison.

Tears sprang into my eyes. I was overtired and stressed by the long wait but they came also from real grief for poor belligerent Ushiwa and for Satoshi, confined in this terrible place and facing the death penalty. I stood and wept, unable to control myself, and maybe my state aroused some spark of humanity in the official. He reached out and rapidly took the bundle and the letter (and the remainder of the small coins I had proferred with them) and slipped them under the desk, making an impatient gesture to me to leave.

It really irked me that he or some other guard would be wearing my gloves and my muffler in the coming winter. I got home very late, frozen to the bone and deeply depressed. I had a vague impression in my head that prisons in the past, while still appalling, had been more porous, less completely cut off from the rest of society. I was sure people used to be able to visit their relatives, take food to them, expect results if they gave bribes. I didn't know where this idea had come from, probably some story I had heard or read. I was horrified that the world had changed so much and disgusted with myself for not noticing.

Once in the world of fairytales the gods watched over human beings, rewarded the generous and the good and punished the greedy. Now those gods had been recruited into the service of the nation, to confirm our Emperor's divinity, our special rights and our sacred mission. But gods were like stories; they could not be forced. As Tensa had said, stories would die on us and I was afraid the gods would too.

I MUST HAVE CAUGHT a cold on my way home from the prison for I was unwell for several days, coughing a lot, my nose stuffed up, and sleeping badly. I made notes of the stories the old man had told me and wrote a new version of 'The Little Sparrow' with my lying but poetic landlady as the villainess. I looked again at my French stories, feeling there was no reason why I should not tell them, and all the time my mind was going over ways I might do something to help Satoshi.

Lying sleepless one night I wondered if I should seek out Jack Green. He had offered to help me with performing, but perhaps he would have some ideas on what had become my main concern. Then my mind slipped into a fantasy about a story thief, like one of the famous robbers of old Edo, who broke into the storehouses of storytellers' minds, carried away their precious material and sold it to untalented hacks in illicit dens in the back streets of the city. An old man, his two sons-in-law and a young foreign storyteller joined forces to outwit them and rescue their beloved tales. There were sword fights and scenes with ninja, one of them a woman, like the one who had attacked me.

Swords.

I was more than a little feverish but I saw lucidly that the only person I knew who could help Satoshi was Takayuki. And I still had in my possession something that I knew was precious to him. I would have to go and bargain with him.

In the morning, between fits of coughing, I told Tae my tale about the story thief (she thought it might work), and then I remembered I had never told her about Jack Green's offer, or his questions about our daughter.

Sei   You know I saw Jack after Tensa's performance? He said he wanted to work more closely with me, even ally himself with our family.

Tae   What exactly did he mean by that?

Sei   It seems he has feelings for Shigure.

Tae   How extraordinary!

Sei   I told him it was hopeless and that she does not want to be married to anyone. Once she is divorced she is determined to live as a single woman and a writer.

Tae   I'm glad you made that clear. We don't want her breaking anyone else's heart.

I'd thought Shigure was shut away in her room but I'd underestimated a daughter's ability to hear her parents talking about her from any part of the house. She almost fell down the stairs and burst into the kitchen.

Shigure   What are you saying about me and Jack Green?

Tae   Your father explained that you don't want to be married, that we are seeking a divorce so you can stay at home and write. It's a ridiculous idea in my opinion but you could at least be grateful to him.

Shigure   But why were you talking about that subject with him, Father?

Sei   He offered to help me out and said he would like to be part of our family. Of course it could be a great help to him – our name has been famous for generations, after all.

Shigure   So it was all about you and him? Nothing about me?

Sei   Well, he intimated he would not be averse to marrying you if that were an option but I said it certainly wasn't. You had made your decision.

Shigure   Why did you say that? You had no right to speak for me!

Tae   No right? He is your father! Anyway, he was only saying what you have repeated endlessly to us.

Shigure   I didn't know . . . Oh, why are you so cruel to me? Always interfering, always doing your best to ruin my life!

She ran out of the room sobbing. Tae and I gazed at each other speechless.

Tae   She had better marry someone soon and move out or I'll end up throttling her!

She picked up her basket, announced she was going shopping and left with the usual excessive clattering that accompanied her rages.

I took the opportunity to climb into the rafters and take down the sword I had hidden there. I knew Tae would prevent me from going out and I knew I would let her persuade me all too readily, for the idea of confronting Takayuki in his own den and offering to trade his sword for a life filled me with terror. I had to leave before she got back. The only thing that kept me going was the fact that I felt so ill death would be a welcome deliverance. At least I wouldn't spend another night racking my burning lungs.

The sky was the colour of lead. It looked as if it might snow, even though it was only the beginning of December. If I walked slowly, my feet froze; if I walked fast, I coughed. Either way the raw air made my eyes and nose water.

It was Sunday, the Western day of rest, which was slowly catching on in the capital, even though most shops stayed open seven days a week. Somewhere a church bell was ringing and there were many foreigners out, riding in rickshaws or walking with their pet dogs. I knew where Takayuki lived for I had seen him coming out of his house several months before. It was a large place in Tsukiji, not far from the water, surrounded by a white wall roofed with tiles that enclosed a beautiful old garden with a stream, a pond, carefully pruned trees, their trunks and boughs wrapped against the cold, rocks and stone lanterns. On that dull day I felt I was entering another world, leaving the modern city behind.

The gate was unbarred and I called out as I went through it but no one answered and I thought the house might be empty.

I was half-relieved but desperation for Satoshi made me move closer and call again. There was the sound of footsteps and a maid appeared, a woman of about thirty who looked as if she might double as a bodyguard for she was strongly built and tall. She resembled one of those women who ran fish cooperatives and everyone called *aneki* – sister boss.

I knew at once she was the woman who had attacked me.

I was trembling as I said my name (unnecessarily, as she knew very well who I was) and asked to see Takayuki. She regarded me with a grave expression, turned her eye on my long bundle and told me to come in and wait by the brazier.

I was already casting her in the role of my story thief. She was certainly an expert in several martial arts, armed and unarmed. She would lie for her master and protect him with her life. Her lover would be the other tattooed thug who had beaten me up. There were probably concealed weapons and booby traps all over the house.

I noticed three pairs of shoes in the entrance hall: fur boots that looked distinctly foreign to me – I wondered if they might be Korean – and one pair of high clogs, like a geisha's or an actor's. An idea suggested itself to me and while I sat by the brazier I entertained myself with a conversation between the shoes. Would left and right boot quarrel like siblings and how would they feel about their owner's feet? I thought I could make it quite humorous.

'Aneki' came back with a tray on which stood a steaming bowl of tea. She told me Lord Yamagishi was home: he was busy for a little while but would be most grateful if I would do him the honour of waiting. In the meantime she had prepared something special for my cold. Her speech was even more old-fashioned than her master's making her sound as if she had just stepped out of some ancient chronicle.

The tea tasted of licorice, ginger and sugar along with some other flavours I did not recognise. I wondered if she was poisoning me but, as I have said, I was rather indifferent to death that day. The bowl was one of those rough-shaped pieces of Hagi ware that were family heirlooms, worth more than I earned in a year. Just holding it in my hands was an aesthetic pleasure, only slightly marred by my fear of breaking it. If it was to be my last drink, it was not a bad one.

From far away I could hear the murmur of voices. There was something strange about their pattern and after a while I realised what it might be – a foreign language. One person, possibly two, were speaking in Korean (a pure guess on my part, inspired by the boots). A third (Kyu?) was translating, while Takayuki (presumably) replied in Japanese.

I finished the tea with no ill effects. Aneki returned and without a word took up the boots and carried them away. The Koreans were to leave by another exit. I felt quite smart to have deduced so much. The tea had soothed my throat and chest in a remarkable way, and when finally Aneki showed me into Takayuki's study, I had regained some confidence.

We passed through the main ten-mat reception room; in one corner there was a large statue of a horse carved from reddish wood, and in the alcove a scroll, inscribed with a winter poem, and a vase holding a stem of susuki grass, dull gold in colour, and a beautifully shaped branch with two scarlet maple leaves clinging to it. The next room was a wide passage that had been turned into a sort of gallery, with rows of woodblock prints along both walls, vibrant with colour, predominantly red; they depicted scenes of battle, warriors and soldiers, not only from the past but also modern ones in smart uniforms with warships flying the red sun flag in the background.

At the end of the passage was the study. Takayuki sat cross-legged on the floor next to a small writing desk while Kyu lounged on a cushion to his right. Behind them the room gave on to the garden, though the screens were closed on this cold morning. The other walls were lined with piles of books, newspapers and magazines. Kyu looked sulky and ducked his head briefly at me without smiling. Takayuki's expression was unreadable but I felt something pent up inside him, like a spring about to uncoil.

Aneki slid the screen door closed behind me. I placed the sword, still wrapped in its bundle, next to me and bowed deeply to Takayuki. My heart had begun to pound again. Takayuki did not look at the sword but I had no doubt he knew immediately what it was.

For a few moments none of us spoke. Takayuki's presence in his own home, surrounded by his treasures, was more powerful, and Kyu looked more beautiful than ever. The knowledge that these two men had been lovers, possibly still were, excited me, not really sexually but deep in the narrative source of my being. Takayuki had been prepared to sacrifice this boy in the pursuit of his cause. And now what was he plotting with the Koreans that he needed Kyu to interpret?

He was manipulative and ruthless yet he was not cold. Beneath his acts lay depths of emotion that he would plumb to the full, like the Mongol chiefs who wept with pity as they had their enemies flayed alive, an unequalled, gut-wrenching mingling of horror, compassion, revenge and pleasure. This was what kabuki portrayed in its greatest moments, those moments that held audiences spellbound and woke ghosts.

Then I knew how I must plead for Satoshi.

Takayuki　　Master, it's good of you to honour us with a visit, especially when you are not well, I believe.

Sei　　Thank you. Because of my cold I will not stay long and I will not waste time. I have come to ask a favour from you, regarding Okuda Satoshi, who was inadvertently caught up in recent events in Chichibu and is awaiting trial in Kosuge prison.

Takayuki　　Okuda was not 'caught up in recent events' as you put it. He went there with a known agitator, bent on taking part in armed insurrection. He had already come to the attention of the authorities for expressing treasonous opinions against the Emperor. Is there any reason why he should not face trial and receive a just punishment?

Sei　　He is a young man of great talent. His main reason for travelling was to see his family. If he has made mistakes, broken the law, of course he should pay for that. I am asking you to save his life. If he dies your revenge is short-lived; in prison, in exile, it will continue forever, made sweeter by your mercy.

Takayuki　　We can always rely on you to obscure the subject with fabrications, Master! I know a great deal more about Okuda than you do. His crimes are against the state. There is nothing personal in the process against him. Why do you talk of revenge?

Sei　　I think you know why.

Takayuki　　I am grateful to you for returning to me something of value. But really nothing prevents me from taking it from you. What will you have to bargain with then?

Sei   I might explain how it came to be in my hands, where it was found. Not widely, of course. Just here in this room.

Takayuki   I could silence you before you had a chance to speak.

Sei   Not very honourable to attack an old man like myself.

Takayuki   Everything I do is honourable because it is in the service of the Emperor.

Sei   Shall I tell Kyu where the sword was found?

Takayuki   Personally I would prefer swift death to years of imprisonment or exile.

Sei   Listen carefully, my audience.

Takayuki   He will be sent to Kushiro. He will die in Hokkaido.

Sei   He will have a chance to live.

Takayuki   You have more nerve than I thought, Master. Very well, give me the sword. I will ask for the death sentence to be commuted to exile. When Michi is living here with me, I will think of him from time to time. He will probably be praying for death.

Sei   I am deeply grateful, Lord.

To be addressed in this feudal manner seemed to please him and his face softened as I passed the sword across the small space between us. He unwrapped it, smiling slightly at the stage scabbard, and drew it out. For a moment I imagined it coming to life and slicing through my flesh. I clenched my sphincter muscles, bringing on a fit of coughing. Takayuki placed the sword next to him and bowed formally to me.

Takayuki   Go back to your storytelling, Master. Next week everything will have changed. My sword returns to me at this time for a purpose. There are powers greater than us that rule our lives and they have used you to bring me a clear sign. It is the time for swords, no longer for words. You stick to your tales of old Japan and I will deal with Korea.

I bowed and thanked him again. Aneki appeared as if by some magic communication and led me back to the front entrance. She told me she was looking forward to my next performance as she was a huge fan. Fascinating as she was, I hoped it would not be a performance she took part in.

THE EFFECTS OF the tea had worn off; the cold air hit
my lungs and a little way down the street I was seized
by another bout of coughing. I stood fighting for breath and
wheezing and, through the noise I was making, heard the rapid
clack of clogs as Kyu arrived beside me.

Kyu   What was all that about? How did you come to
have Takayuki's sword?

Sei   I can't tell you.

Kyu   You were ready to a few minutes ago. But your
silence was worth something to him. Why?

Sei   He paid for my silence. I can't go back on that
transaction.

Kyu   Well, I haven't got time to talk about it. Can
you take a message to Kat'chan for me?

Sei   Now? I am not well, as you can see. I have to go home.

Kyu   It's important and I can't go myself. There is no time. We are leaving tonight.

Sei   Leaving? Where are you going? And what about the play?

Kyu   I can't tell you where. Say I am ill, say I caught your cold. I probably will catch it now. I don't want to go, I would far rather be in the theatre tomorrow night than in . . . but I must not tell you!

Sei   Let me guess. Seoul?

Kyu   Don't breathe a word to anyone! I have to go with Takayuki. I have to do what he asks of me. I told you once before, I owe him my life. Please tell Kat'chan. I hope I will be back soon.

I agreed reluctantly. It was not far out of my way but I did not want to pass on my cold to my grandsons and I was longing to get home. However if someone did not warn Kat'chan, the play would be in trouble so I resigned myself to my errand. I tried to raise my spirits by concentrating on Satoshi, but really what had I achieved? An unreliable assurance from Takayuki of a long exile in a place far colder than Tokyo.

When I arrived, Kat'chan was out. Yuri greeted me with some concern and made me sit at the hearth, telling me he had gone to church with the boys. Her tone suggested she was not happy about it.

Sei   You don't share his interest in Christianity?

Yuri   I don't know what's happened to him, to be

honest. He's no longer the man I married. In some ways he's more considerate – he doesn't lose his temper so much – but I miss the old Kat'chan. I don't know why he wants to change anything. Things are fine how they are. Sure, the theatre is stressful but it's what he's grown up with. It's his life. Already Fusao wants to do the same work. Kat'chan would be throwing away generations of tradition if he leaves the Shintomi-za.

Sei　　　　He's seriously thinking of leaving the theatre?

Yuri　　　　He wants us all to join the church and be baptised, and dedicate ourselves to the work of Jesus.

Sei　　　　It all sounds so drastic. Can't he just go to church, sing a few hymns or whatever they do?

Yuri　　　　It's an all-or-nothing religion. You're either in or out, for or against. No half-measures.

I had an awful presentiment that Yuri was going to want a divorce and come home too.

Sei　　　　I suppose you have to do what he wants; he is your husband, after all.

Yuri　　　　Father! I expected better from you. Shouldn't I make my own decisions in this? It's my soul, *after all*! Don't worry, we aren't going to descend on you permanently any time soon, even though the boys love being with you and Mother.

Sei　　　　What about the boys? Who decides for them?

Yuri　　　　They like the stories. They adore their father. They will want to do whatever he does. When I think of them I feel I will have to go along with it, to keep my family together.

But won't God know I am not really a believer? You know all my life I've hated deception and lies.

Sei   As a little girl you were always the one who wanted to know, 'Is it true?' I suspected that you did not really care for stories.

Yuri   I used to believe every word you said. And then I found out you made up stories for a living. After that I never trusted them. And now I keep asking myself that very question: is it true? What makes Jesus more true than Shaka? We are told to forget Buddhism and believe in the old Way of the Gods. Then Christianity comes along and tells us those gods are evil. But I grew up with all those *kami*. I can't make them disappear from my life. And who is telling me the truth?

She stared at me for a moment but I could see she did not really expect an answer, which was just as well as I had none. She made me some hot gruel with an egg whisked through it, and while I was slurping it up Kat'chan and the boys returned. Soji immediately began telling me a story he had heard in church about a lost sheep, with Fusao adding his own embellishments. Even though I was born in the year of the Sheep, none of us had ever seen a real one, nor had any idea what the work of caring for them might involve. That was no hindrance to my grandsons' imaginations.

When they had finished I told Kat'chan why I had come and he swore in exasperation, making me think that the old Kat'chan was not too far away, but then he composed his features and closed his eyes as if listening to an inner voice.

Kat'chan   It must be some sort of message from God. What does he want me to do?

Yuri   Contact the understudy, I imagine, so he is prepared for tomorrow's performance.

Kat'chan   I'll do that, of course. I'll go after we've eaten. But overall, in the long run, what does it mean? Am I to leave the theatre too?

We were all quite unable to answer. Yuri wanted me to stay for the midday meal but the gruel had satisfied my meagre appetite so I left Kat'chan to his contemplation of the inscrutable mind of God and went home, wondering why Takayuki was taking Kyu to Seoul and what would happen there.

What happened became known to history as the Kōshin coup, instigated by Kim Ok-gyun and other Korean patriots. It took place in Seoul on the night of December 5th, though we did not hear about it in Tokyo until days later and most people never heard the details I learned. I thought of it as one of my secret stories, recorded in my journal but never to be told on stage. It was recounted to me by Kyu – what a master of narrative he was! Under different circumstances he might have become my disciple; I might have adopted him and given him the name Akabane. He came to my house one night about a week later, on his way home from the theatre. I invited him in and he sat down by the hearth, where Shigure tried not to stare at him too openly. I suggested it was time for her to go to bed. Tae bustled about in the kitchen while Kyu talked to me.

Kyu   I came to thank you for taking my message to Kat'chan.

Sei   Well, Kat'chan is my son-in-law, as you know. I did it as much for his sake as for yours. I suppose you are back in the theatre?

Kyu   I had to put up with a scolding, but everyone was glad to see me. Without me the play is not as good.

Sei   No doubt that's true. I hope you won't make a habit of disappearing.

Kyu   I hope I never have to disappear for such a reason again. I have lived through a nightmare. You like stories, don't you, Master? Shall I make you a gift of this one? To repay you for the favour you did for me? I've read what the journalists say in the newspaper reports but they only tell part of it. They were not there.

Sei   I would like to hear it.

Kyu   It was a bitterly cold night. Winter had already swept down from the north. Everything was frozen. All the great gates closed at dusk. The city of Seoul was dark and silent, the streets deserted, even the cats and dogs were hiding beneath the house floors.

A banquet was being held to celebrate the opening of the Telegraph and Post Office. Chief Minister Min Yong-ik had recently returned from America. Oh America! How I wish I could go there! The minister had ideas on how to reform the government but the Chinese, meddling as usual, had persuaded Queen Min to force him to abandon them.

Sei   There were Chinese troops stationed just outside Seoul, people are saying.

Kyu   That is why the Queen was so confident. She

knew she could call on them at any time. But we did not know
that. We were waiting at the legation with the Japanese soldiers
until a message came that Kim had struck against the minister.
Then we raced through the empty streets to join him.

It was like a scene from a play – the darkened palace, the
lanterns, the drawn swords, the ministers arriving in their
chairs put to death one after another as they passed through
the gates. I saw Takayuki's sword take life over and again, the
blood, real blood, flowing dark and sticky, not spurting red as
it does on the stage. It was the sword you gave back to him
which he took as a sign that the time to act had come, that
victory was certain. There was a moment when it seemed to
be true. Kim Ok-gyun sat in the palace already writing bills of
reform. But then the Chinese came, we had to flee and the city
itself erupted against us. Fires burst out, drums were pounding,
stones came hurtling out of the darkness, along with iron pots
and lids, burning torches. I thought we would die there.

Sei   I heard many did die.

Kyu   At least forty dead were left behind and their
bodies were chopped into pieces and fed to dogs in the streets.
Somehow we got onto a Japanese steamer and sailed away,
taking Kim with us. Will he ever be able to return? Queen
Min's agents will hunt him down and kill him. I am afraid they
will do the same to me. Where can I hide? Everyone knows
my face now.

Sei   I hope you will not be in any danger. There's a
lot of impassioned talk about punishing Korea, going to war
with China and so on. Feelings are running high.

Kyu   On both sides. The Japanese despise the Koreans
and the Koreans hate the Japanese, with more reason, I think

– do you know why? Because your government has allowed such riffraff to flock there. If your concern is to help Korea reform, why didn't you send us doctors or teachers instead of illegal land surveyors, counterfeiters, corrupt merchants and other ruffians who cheat and exploit us? Why doesn't your government negotiate openly instead of carrying on plots and intrigues with every unscrupulous villain who wants to make a quick fortune?

I had no answer to these questions, the machinations of the government being as unfathomable to me as the mind of God.

Sei   Takayuki was unharmed? He also returned safely?

Kyu   He is disappointed that it is all over. He was hoping for war.

Sei   He will not be satisfied until he gets it. But beware, he will sacrifice you to his cause.

Kyu   That may indeed be my fate.

JUST BEFORE THE end of the year I received a letter from Satoshi that told me Takayuki had honoured his part in our transaction.

My dear Master,
I am writing to you on your gift of paper. I was told that you came to the prison. I am more grateful than I can express not only for the paper and ink but for the fact you came so far to show me I was not forgotten.

I am allowed to write one letter before I leave in the New Year and I have chosen to write to you because I know you will fulfil my few wishes. My trial has taken place, along with so many others. We were not allowed to defend ourselves but were expected to confess our guilt. I was condemned to death but a few days ago was shown great mercy and am to be sent to Kushiro Prison in Hokkaido. It seems it is my destiny to go north after all. My sentence is for at least ten years.

Please keep my books for me. Dispose of my other belongings however you see fit. Keep any money you make from the sale. Inform the language academy of the reasons for my absence and apologise to them. And please tell Michi where I am.

Thank you for your kindness to me and your friendship. The memory of our time with Monsieur Guy will always stay with me,

> *Your friend and colleague,*
> *Okuda Satoshi*

He made no mention of the other gifts; the guards must have kept them for themselves. For a few moments I cursed them passionately but by the time Tae came to ask what on earth was the matter, my anger had dissolved in grief. I handed her the letter, and after she had read it we both wept together. I had told her I had returned the sword, but I did not say it was to Takayuki, nor had we discussed the deal I had made for it. At that moment neither of us expected ever to see Satoshi again.

Later that afternoon, Shigure came with me to Hirano's to start packing up Satoshi's belongings. There was a smart black rickshaw with cinnamon-coloured trimmings waiting outside. I spoke to Chie and told her the news; she said she would take Shigure to the room and help her.

Sei　　　I must also inform Miss Itasaki.

Chie   She's in her room. Tell her the rickshaw is waiting for her, will you?

I called quietly at Michi's door. She slid it open as if she had been on the point of leaving. For a moment I did not recognise her. She was, as I had never seen her before, wearing a Western dress, a deep blue satin gown cut to reveal her white throat and neck, the fabric clinging to her breasts, defining her slender waist and then cascading around her to the floor. Round that fragile throat sparkled a diamond necklace. On the clothes rack was a white fur stole. She smelled strongly of the same fragrance she had worn before, on the night of Satoshi's lecture – the expensive one.

She smiled at my expression. I must have been staring open-mouthed.

Michi   I am going to the Deer Cry Pavilion, to a ball. I'm nervous – it's the first time I've worn these clothes.

Sei   I have had a letter from Satoshi. He wanted you to know the verdict of his trial. He is to be exiled.

Her face had been flushed slightly with excitement but now the colour drained from it. She took the letter from me and read it as if she could suck his presence from it. While she read it over and over I gazed around her room. The expensive dress, the fur, the jewels, the mirror with its make-up boxes and bottles contrasted strangely with the piles of medical books around the writing desk and Michi's plain old clothes – which I realised I had not seen her in for some time – folded neatly on the floor.

On the little writing desk, among her notebooks, lay a small sequined purse, such as Western women carried, and next to it, waiting to be placed inside, a white handkerchief, some coins and a glass bottle of the same brilliant blue as her dress. My eye was drawn to it by its colour and the unusual ridges down its side. I imagined it was the perfume.

Michi lowered the letter and looked at me.

Michi   Twelve years! But at least he will not die.

Sei   For which we have to thank Takayuki.

Michi   And you. He told me you went to see him. It was brave of you. I am very grateful.

Sei   I did not do it for you alone. I did it for Satoshi, and of course for my own peace of mind.

Michi   You must think I have become very selfish. For some reason it pains me if you think ill of me. I suppose because you are a storyteller and I feel as if you are recording my life. I don't want to look bad in your story.

She glanced around the room and picked up the bottle, putting it into the purse along with her other things. With a flash, I realised what it was – it was poison, the brilliant blue colour, the ridged sides, designed to warn of its deadly content. I stared at Michi, wondering if she really was a poison woman as I had once imagined, and wondering to what extent I had created her.

Michi   You are writing about me, aren't you?

Sei   I don't think badly of you, far from it. I admire you very much. But I suppose I wish your life had turned out differently. I am afraid of what Takayuki will demand of you.

Michi   I cannot refuse him. You are not the only one who made a trade for Satoshi's life. And he needs me, now more than ever.

Sei   After what happened in Seoul?

Michi   It was a debacle. He was badly affected. He saw many close friends die, and they could not even retrieve the bodies. He thinks an opportunity to install a new government in Korea, one more favourable to the Japanese, has been lost, and Kim Ok-gyun was betrayed by the Foreign Minister, Inoue Kaoru. We spoke of him once before, do you remember?

Sei   I beg you, don't let Takayuki use you to get revenge.

Michi   Do you think I am going to poison the minister?

Sei   You told me once you wanted to kill him.

Michi   Well, maybe I will.

Sei   Your rickshaw is waiting.

Michi   I wish I did not have to go. I am too sad now. But Takayuki is expecting me. Do you understand, Storyteller, how a man's need for a woman binds her to him? Don't forget to put that in your story.

She pulled the fur from the rack and draped it over her shoulders. It framed her face as if she were a snow woman. If her heart was broken, she gave no sign of it.

I hardly dared think about Michi and the poison and the Foreign Minister in case I gave life to my fears. I scanned the newspapers every day looking for reports of an assassination but nothing appeared, and the oblivious Inoue continued his round of discussions, diplomacy, balls and bazaars. A treaty was signed with Korea making reparations for the burned legation and the Japanese dead, but anti-Korean feeling still smouldered in Tokyo, as presumably anti-Japanese feeling did in Seoul.

I rewrote 'The History of a Nose' and made the old priest a mountain goblin, a *tengu*, and the owner of the nose a *tanuki*, the animal rascal hero of many a folk tale. I set the story in the mountains and embellished it with descriptions of the *tanuki*'s cunning and thievery. It became something of a comedy – a *tanuki*'s nose is undeniably droll and the idea of a *tengu* amassing a mountain of them was hilarious. I had moved into fantasy to give utterance to the unspeakable so everyone could endure it – both audience and authorities. I thought in this way I might satisfy the lot of them, but what about the source of my story, my visitant, the priest Keinen?

One day I lifted the floorboards to check on the diary. It was not there.

My first thought was that we had been robbed – maybe even by my story thief? I shuddered to think of Aneki creeping silently into my house at night. Why had Aka not barked? What else might she have stolen? My head was a treasure-house of ideas these days. When I voiced my fears to Tae, she told me she had taken the diary to the local temple because it gave her the creeps. The priest was an old friend of her father and he performed a blessing on it and put it away in the storehouse with copies of the Lotus Sutra in Prince Shotoku's hand, a sandal that had belonged to Kōbō Daishi, the tail of a flying horse, an old water clock, some cups said to be pure gold and so on and so on.

I hoped Keinen found peace among those holy relics. Sometimes I went to the temple and tried to explain to him that I had done my best, had been beaten up, placed under a ban and reduced to poverty. I prayed that the cruelties of the past would never happen again, though without much optimism, for Takayuki's words kept echoing through my head. *It is the time for swords, no longer for words.* And what else had he said? *It is better to be cruel than weak.* I prayed that my country would not take that path.

Keinen made no response.

S HIGURE FINALLY FINISHED a story that she would allow to be published and it appeared in *Modern Days* just before the early spring festival of Setsubun. It was another drama of modern life, told with deep insight and delicacy, combining old poetic imagery with a modern setting and characters that might have started out based on Shigure and Renzō but had taken on a life of their own and become real people. I felt so much for them I really wanted them to overcome their mutual misunderstanding and be reconciled. I was devastated at the end of the story when the husband, Tasuke, died.

My wife took the story as proof that Shigure regretted leaving her husband and wanted to return to him.

Shigure   It's just fiction, Mother! It's what might have been . . . but these people are not real. Tasuke is not Renzō.

Tae   Well, Renzō's going to think he is and so are a lot of other people.

Shigure   Why does everyone have to be so literal? Father, you understand, don't you?

Sei   I suppose I do. But Renzō could be an essential part of your writing, like the grit in the oyster, the irritation that produces the pearl. Life can never be perfectly arranged and it's the imperfections that are the raw material of storytelling. You will never find a more compliant husband. Don't throw that away heedlessly.

Tae   You must want to go back in your heart or you would not write such a story. Don't let your pride get in the way.

Shigure   It is not pride. I can never be reconciled with Renzō. Why can't you understand me?

And once again she left the room in tears.

Tae thought she was weakening and kept up her nagging, with some support from me. I began to think the marriage might be saved but the story proved itself to be true in a way we had not expected. Renzō returned to his office late one night to collect some documents and surprised a thief. Foolishly, he tackled the intruder and was stabbed in the stomach. His secretary found his body in the morning.

There was some rather unpleasant publicity. Renzō's family blamed Shigure, would not speak to us at the funeral and declared since they were estranged she would inherit nothing. I felt curiously responsible too, as if my story thief had come to life and committed murder. Shigure wept for days but it was hard to tell if it was remorse or real grief or even relief. She gained an unfortunate reputation and several people asked her if she would write the death of their husband or mother-in-law. It seemed a convenient way to get rid of people. I thought it would make a marvellous horror story, and filed it away in my mind until my daughter was less sensitive about the subject. Sales of that edition of *Modern Days* were unprecedented. Shigure swore she would never write another word, but naturally none of us believed her.

Next, another story bore fruit, the one Tensa was still performing daily at the Aosora, but as so often happens, in a way no one had predicted. Yuri brought the children for Setsubun and we all took part in throwing beans and shouting, *Luck In! Demons Out!* as tradition demanded. Shigure walked home with them, and after they left Tae and I talked about the children in the way grandparents do, admiring their intelligence, sweet nature and so on and so on

Sei   It's a shame we have only the two boys. I wish there were more babies coming along.

Tae   You know Teru is expecting a child?

Sei   Know? How should I know when no one tells me anything?

Tae   You would know more about your own family if you paid attention instead of always being lost in your world of make-believe.

Sei   My make-believe, as you call it, is our only lifeline. If I cannot write and perform there is no income – end of story!

Tae   I suppose you will perform again one day, and we will have some income. We have to keep hoping. Anyway, I am telling you now. The baby is due in the autumn.

Sei   Heavens, Tensa didn't waste any time! Now why couldn't he have just done that in the first place and saved us all that heartache?

Tae   The thing is . . . don't be angry . . . I have to tell you . . .

Sei   Eh?

Tae   Tensa is not the father. It is Yūdai's child.

Sei   Yūdai? The musician? Tensa's partner?

Tae   Yes, and they are all happy about it, so there is no need to interfere.

Sei   Who said I was going to interfere? I'm just surprised, not angry. Actually it's the funniest thing I've heard in a long time!

Tae   And you are not to turn it into a story!

Sei   I can't promise that! How did it come about? Does Yūdai have a thing for cats?

Tae   She didn't dress up as a cat. That would be ridiculous. But she used the boy disguise; she spoke in men's language, tied her hair up in a ponytail and did the housework in leggings and a jacket. Apparently Tensa didn't know what to make of it and his poor old mother was completely confused, but Yūdai was entranced. He's always liked women as much as men and, well, there you are!

Sei   Isn't Tensa jealous?

Tae   He was at first but Teru says Yūdai still loves him. He just likes her as well. And now she's pregnant and she's happy. But don't breathe a word to anyone. To the world it will be Tensa's child.

Sei   Does Shigure know the truth?

Tae   I believe Shigure planned the whole thing. She didn't seem in the least surprised when I told her.

Sei   I hope you told her not to write about it.

Tae   You know she never intends to write again.

Sei   She won't be able to help herself.

One more story was unfolding, one more baby on the way. A few days later, Michi called at the house. It was a chilly day, but with more than a hint of spring. The plum tree in our garden was flowering and the narcissus Tae grew in pots round the entrance were just beginning to bud.

There were plum blossoms too on Michi's silk kimono.

Michi   I am leaving Hirano's, Master. I have come to say goodbye and to thank you for all your kindness.

Sei   There's nothing to thank me for. You were more kind to me, taking the time to listen to an old man, patching me up when I was falling to pieces. Are you going back to Yamaguchi? Are there problems at home?

Michi   I am not going so far away. I don't know that I will ever see my family again. I don't dare even write to them. I've let them down.

Sei   What's happened? You are not abandoning your studies?

Michi   Dr Kida has dismissed me. A bottle of poison went missing. He suspected me of stealing it. He would have overlooked it if I had given in to his demands but I refused. So now I have no teacher and he will make sure I never find another one.

Sei   But all your plans, your dreams . . .

Michi   Were they really my dreams or were they what my mother decided for me? I would never have passed the second stage of the exam. It was too difficult for me. I am sure we will meet . . . in fact I will be living not far away, in Tsukiji.

Sei   With Takayuki?

Michi   Yes, with Takayuki. We will be married. I am carrying his child. There is no reason why we should not marry – we are both widowed. He desperately wants a son and I believe the child is a boy. I already dream about him as he grows inside me. You know, I have many brothers and sisters whom I hardly know. We rarely saw them when I was growing up. My mother, who adopted me, was so strict, so ambitious for me. When my husband died the only thing she said was, 'Now you will be able to go to Tokyo and study.' I know she meant well, but I never had a chance to recover from grief. I think it was grief that drew me to Takayuki. He calmed my body and made me forget.

Sei   He will make a prisoner of you.

Michi   It's no more than I deserve, my punishment for betraying Satoshi. I might as well be in prison since he is lost to me.

Sei   And the poison? Did you steal it?

Michi   You know I did, Master. You saw it.

Sei   I thought I might have imagined it. I seem to be doing that a lot lately. My eyes play tricks on me.

Michi   I took it. I wanted to murder Inoue Kaoru. I blamed him for the disaster in Seoul, for Takayuki's despair, for my father's death all those years ago. I was willing to sacrifice my life the night of the ball but the opportunity did not arise. Maybe it will one day. I still have the poison – it is arsenic – but now I have to consider my son's life as well as my own.

She bowed to me gracefully and I went out into the street with her, where the smart black rickshaw was waiting. It was not yet a year since I had first seen her in her plain student garb. That serious young girl was gone forever.

The pain of thinking about what might have been was so strong I had to go to my study immediately and write it all down.

About a month later my manager, Rinjirō, appeared at my house. I had not seen him for weeks, during which time we had been barely surviving. Like everyone in the neighbourhood, we relied on credit from shopkeepers. I owed Hirano almost as much rent as I had last year when Takayuki had paid it for me, and anything we owned of any value was at the pawnshop. Shigure's story kept us going, along with what I could scrounge from Tensa and Kat'chan. Just about the only person I had not approached for a loan was Jack Green. It was weeks since I'd seen him too and I wondered if he had bowed to the wishes of his family and given up performing. He was probably married to a nice young Englishwoman and living on the Bluff in Yokohama, in one of those big bungalows, with a little lapdog; maybe he was writing for the English-language newspapers and taking part in amateur dramatics.

Tae greeted Rinjirō with exaggerated pleasure and surprise, fussing over him excessively and making him quite embarrassed.

Rinjirō   I had not forgotten you, Master. On the contrary, I've been making plans for a new season. I've been to the police every week and I've just been told the ban on you won't be enforced as long as your material is not subversive.

Sei   I've been working on a few things, a new version of 'The Little Sparrow', a *tanuki* story and a modern drama, a love story. Nothing political, all very innocuous.

Rinjirō   I'll book a hall. How soon can you start?

Tae   He can start as soon as the hall is ready. But he'll need an advance.

Rinjirō replied that that would be a bit difficult – after all, our debts from last year's fiasco were still unpaid – but Tae turned her attentions on him even more, made him tea, flattered him and flirted with him, and finally got four yen out of him. I remembered how I had suspected her of having an affair; now I saw the truth. She did it, as she did most things, for me. She might be irritable and annoying, though she had seemed less so recently, but underneath she was completely loyal and devoted. I saw how lost I would be without her and I realised how selfish I had been during our marriage. I did not deserve her. I resolved I would make it up to her in the time we had left together – but after a couple of days of little attentions and kind words, she declared I was making her nervous and begged me to leave her alone and go back to my writing.

So I returned to my story, 'The Silk Kimono'. I had to change my characters, of course, give them new names and disguise them sufficiently so they would not recognise themselves, although it was unlikely that any of them would attend a performance. I suppose I kept some of their essence: Kyu's mystery and exotic sensuality, Satoshi's intellectual curiosity and his sense of humour, Michi's fearlessness and beauty, Takayuki's courage and commitment to the old virtues. I used their voices and their gestures, so familiar to me, actors' slang, French words, medical terms, old-fashioned speech. I filled their lives with complications and intrigues, though I could not reveal Takayuki's true conspiracies in Korea, nor was I ever able to solve the mystery surrounding the deaths of his father and brother that he had talked to me about the night we ate *fugu* at the Bakan. Of course I arranged it so that at least one of them died tragically and one acted heroically and so on and so on. A major plot revelation was the silk kimono, a symbol of betrayal, the gift of one lover recognised for its true value by the other. And in a way my ending was the same: my heroine married one man to save the life of another. Which one did she truly love? We would never be sure and nor would they.

The story was a long one and it ran in three episodes. Each night I started with two of my short humorous stories and after the interval I related 'The Silk Kimono'. I loved its characters almost more than my family. I admired their courage, so much more honourable than my own cowardice. Escaping the ordinariness of my own life, I had pursued them like a hunter after prey. They were tigers for me to capture, horses for me to tame. It was a mastery like the act of love, and this must have been evident in the tale for it was a success, as I said, perhaps the greatest success of my life.

Jack Green attended an early performance and came back later with his stenographer. The whole thing was recorded in shorthand and transformed into print. A newspaper published it as a serial and later it was turned into a book. Suddenly I had become a novelist. I began to make money. Tae repaid most of our debts but not the rent, for the Hiranos were, she said, relatives and would never demand it. Chie came to hate us almost as much as she hated her husband and took to preparing special delicacies for us to demonstrate her displeasure and disappointment.

Jack had not given up performing as I had thought but had been away in England. He told me he thought he should try life there but he had missed everything about Japan and had made the decision to return. He said he wanted to settle down and gave a deep sigh, an exact replica of the sigh Shigure gave during the interval at Tensa's performance.

Jack was a frequent visitor and Aka no longer barked savagely at him but greeted him with the excited yelp he reserved for members of the family. From this as much as from the sigh, I understood it was only a matter of time before Shigure admitted her true feelings to herself and the rest of us, and Jack Green became my fourth – or maybe fifth, if I counted Yūdai – son-in-law.

ᴬFTER THE WEDDING Jack moved in with us. He took care of the business side of things and I made even more money, enough to buy a house not far away, still in Kyōbashi and large enough for two families. My wife ran the household and now had three writers to look after. She still grumbled all the time but the money coming in helped to soften her temper. Teru had a baby girl, followed quickly by a son. Tensa was not exactly a doting father, though he found the children amusing, but Uncle Yūdai made up for that. And I heard, though I had not seen her, that Michi also gave birth to a boy, the son Takayuki so desired. The following year Shigure found time between writing two very successful novels to bring another baby girl into our family.

You might think that was the ending, a happy one of success, marriage and children. It was like one of the stories I told that everyone wanted to hear, tales of the triumph of love and courage, the overcoming of frailty and stupidity, where luck befell the good, generosity was rewarded and greed punished. In the years that followed I told many of these – luckily I now had access to a vast new supply of material. Jack had brought recently published books from England and we worked on these together – stories of pirates and hidden treasure, a famous outlaw who stole from the rich to give to the poor, a father and son who magically swapped their physical appearance and ended up understanding each other a little better. I particularly liked this last one, which lent itself to a great deal of comedy when we reset it in present-day Tokyo, a city full of fathers and sons locked in mutual incomprehension.

But there were still stories I could not tell, not because they were unpopular but because, no matter how true they were, they had to be kept secret. If I spoke them aloud, either the authorities would ban them, and me, or I would be silenced, intimidated, beaten up again, or if I persisted, removed permanently from the stage.

My life was sweet and I did not want to leave it. So like Keinen I kept a diary, this journal, where I hoarded not only the account of how I came to write 'The Silk Kimono', along with fragments of ideas – shoes, sighs, dogs and so on and so on – but also fully fledged stories, true accounts that I felt compelled to record even if they would never be allowed out into the light. Sometimes I sensed Keinen beside me encouraging me: *write it down. You never know whose eyes will discover it years into the future.*

The months and the years spun past as fast and as blurred as a children's pinwheel whirling in the wind. Bicycles appeared on the streets as if by magic – one week none, the next hundreds – followed by electric lights. The Shintomi-za adopted evening performances and Western-style seating; shipwrecks occurred, murders, earthquakes, volcanic eruptions; the railway thrust out beside the old Tōkaidō and the Emperor progressed along it in his state carriage; the Empress put on Western clothes.

My son-in-law Kat'chan continued to struggle between his first love, kabuki, and the new seduction of Christianity. His church had contacts in Hokkaido and he began to travel there every summer, sometimes taking his family with him now the boys were growing older, sometimes travelling alone and coming back with new tales of incomparable mountain peaks and tantalising snippets of Ainu legends.

I often asked him if he had heard any news of Satoshi, not very hopefully as Hokkaido was a huge, wild place and Kushiro was far from Hakodate. He would reply that he had asked the congregation to include him in their prayers, and I believe he too prayed for Satoshi.

Kat'chan   Come with me sometime, Master. You would find these native people and their stories fascinating and perhaps you will find Satoshi.

Sei   It is a long journey for an old man. I suppose one day you will go and live there.

Kat'chan   I would love to do missionary work, but how can the Shintomi-za run without me?

Sei   It won't be long before Fusao is old enough to take over. He works with you already, doesn't he?

Kat'chan   Yes, and he's impatient to have my job! He can do the technical side without any problem, but he doesn't understand the complexities of theatre and the personalities of actors. He thinks a scientific explanation can be found for everything. You know that vision I had years ago on Mount Yari, the one that made me believe God was calling me?

Sei   How could I forget?

Kat'chan   Fusao found a book at school, *The Wonders of Sea and Sky*, which talks about that phenomenon. Apparently a lot of people see similar things on mountains – it's something to do with the altitude and the sun. It's got a German name – it means 'broken spectre' or something like that.

Sei   Does that affect your faith?

Kat'chan   No, I will always be convinced it was a vision of some sort. I know God is calling me. But I can't leave the theatre now. You'll never guess why.

Sei   Tell me.

Kat'chan   We have been invited to put on a performance for their Imperial Majesties.

Sei   How respectable kabuki has become!

Kat'chan   It is now considered a national treasure. I would never have dreamed of it twenty years ago.

Sei   Surely the Emperor will not attend the theatre?

Kat'chan   No, that would be going too far. The performance is to be in Count Inoue's mansion. Would you like to go? I am allowed to include a few famous artists in the invitations. I am sure you qualify.

I must say, I was flattered and excited. I bought new clothes and made great efforts with my appearance, not that I had much hope of hiding my age. When I arrived and found my seat I saw Michi and Takayuki sitting not far from me, she in the same deep blue Western gown and white fur stole that she had worn the night she slipped the bottle of poison into her sequined purse.

I had not seen them since the success of 'The Silk Kimono', and now watching them felt strange – they seemed both more and less real than my characters. Without being able to help myself, I began to spin another story, a murder mystery of the type that was just beginning to be translated into Japanese from English. 'Death of a Minister', I would call it. The setting was perfect: the elaborate opening ceremony, the chanting of the Shinto priests, the glittering audience, the beautiful woman bent on revenge. Then I realised that just allowing this title into my head was probably treasonous. I glanced towards Takayuki – I think I was afraid he would be looking at me and reading my thoughts. At that moment the Emperor made his appearance and we all stood and bowed deeply.

His Majesty stood next to the Empress in an elevated box decorated with flowers. She wore traditional clothes, I suppose in honour of kabuki, but he was in Western evening dress, with a sash of honour across his chest, and medals on his lapel. It was astonishing to be so close to him. I had seen photographs, of course, but it was the first time I and many in the audience had set eyes on him in the flesh. I found myself trembling. One man not far from me actually fainted and the rest of us had tears in our eyes. I looked back at Takayuki, remembering the meeting I had gone to with him, when the Emperor's photograph had been concealed so no profane eyes would fall on it. I was interested to see if he would look at the Emperor now or if he would turn his gaze away.

I was riveted by what I saw. I could not stop looking at him. For he had gone white, his eyes starting as he stared at the Emperor's face. He was struggling to regain the control he usually held over his emotions, breathing heavily, to the point of sobbing. And still he could not tear his eyes away.

The Emperor sat. The audience followed. The wooden clappers began to beat for the beginning of the play. Takayuki was staring straight ahead, as if looking back years into the past. And suddenly with a flash of insight I knew.

I recalled what he had told me: the unearned respect, the unfailing financial and moral support, his father's death in Kyoto, and his brother's . . . except his brother had not died. They were not his bones crumbling in Ryōzen. He was there before us now, the Son of the Gods. And Takayuki had recognised him.

I could imagine the whole thing. The Emperor's death from smallpox and then the death of his young heir, the panic among the loyalist conspirators, the fear of civil war or anarchy, the search for a suitable sixteen-year-old, the demand made of Takayuki's father, his acquiescence, his last words to his son; surely he would have committed *seppuku*, cut open his belly, in an honourable unknown death? Terauchi, the man I had met at Black Ocean, might even have been his assistant and taken off his head with a sword – possibly the Yamagishi family heirloom that I had hidden in the rafters and traded for my friend Satoshi's life.

Heaven knows whose bones they were in that tomb in Ryōzen – maybe even those of the young heir, Emperor Kōmei's son. A sixteen-year-old boy from Chōshū, a lover of horses, a descendant of the Southern line, had taken his place.

I cursed myself for my foolish ability to see story everywhere. Within a few minutes Takayuki had recovered. No one seemed to have noticed his reaction – everyone was overcome by emotion to some extent. I told myself I had imagined the whole thing. It would be years before my suspicions were confirmed. For some other person had noticed Takayuki, someone who knew the truth and who realised that Takayuki now knew too.

THE LAST TRACES of the old Edo way of life were disappearing. Symbolically our dear dog Aka died in his sleep one night. He was fourteen years old, a fine age for a dog. Tae was distraught and his death left a huge gap in our lives. I kept waking in the night and hearing him give his welcoming yelp; sometimes I was sure he still followed me through the streets. After a few weeks I found another puppy; we called him Aka-chan and he grew up looking and behaving just like the old Aka. It was quite easy to believe he had chosen to be reincarnated one more time as our family dog, amazing us with his devotion and fidelity.

I became an addict of newspapers, mining them daily for snippets to use in my performances. In the spring of 1894 I read reports of the murder of the Korean patriot Kim Ok-gyun.

Since the Kōshin coup ten years before, Kim had been in exile in Japan, but finally he had been persuaded by a man he trusted to go to Shanghai, where a Chinese agent shot him on the orders of Queen Min. His body was sent to Korea, where it was quartered and the pieces dispatched to be exposed in the four corners of the realm.

Like many others I thought Kim had been betrayed by our government and the vindictiveness of the Korean Queen towards the corpse of her enemy made me shudder, but it was not a subject I dared speak of in public, though I recorded all the details I could find in my diary.

I had never spoken to anyone of Kyu's account of the Kōshin coup. As I said, it became one of my secret stories, hidden within the pages of this diary. I had seen Kyu quite often over the years – he still lived at Hirano's, though in a better room now, and he must have looked on me as something of a confidant for he always opened his heart to me as well as gossiping about the theatre. I had of course followed the ups and downs of his career through Kat'chan. The night before he died he came to me with his last story.

It was the second week of October and it had been raining all day. Shigure and Tae had gone with the grandchildren (Shigure had had another baby girl) to listen to Jack's latest performance, but I had been feeling tired and decided not to go with them. I had recently celebrated my sixtieth birthday; I had passed through the entire cycle of years and was back in the *kinoto hitsuji* year, the year of the Sheep, in which I was born.

Kyu wore traditional clothes and carried a large black umbrella which he left open on the verandah. He never seemed to change or age; he still had the large dark eyes, pale skin

243

and red lips he had had as a boy. He was thinner, though, the bones of his skull and face so close to the surface they resembled the sculpted elements of a mask. I took him inside and offered to make tea, but he declined. He seemed nervous and jittery, making me wonder if he was addicted to laudanum, as Kat'chan had told me many actors were – it dulled the pain from arthritis and old injuries. He sat down opposite me and fixed his gaze on me.

Kyu   A letter came for you today from Okuda Satoshi. It had been sent to your old house. I said I would bring it to you. Mr Hirano is not well and Chie is too busy to come herself.

Sei   I have heard nothing from him for years. I thought he must be dead.

Kyu   Go ahead and read it. I can wait.

Sei   No, no, I will read it later. I expect he wants me to send his books to him. I kept them all for him, you know. They have been as if dead, for none of us can read French, but now Satoshi will bring them to life again. I can't tell you how happy I am. Thank you! But why aren't you at the theatre?

Kyu   The only play I appear in these days is *Hideyoshi's Invasion* and that doesn't open again until tomorrow night. I have been away for a week.

He did not seem to want to leave, so I asked a few questions about his life. I gathered from what he told me that he was discouraged and disappointed. Sakutarō had discarded him for a younger boy. His hopes of adoption into a traditional theatre family had never been fulfilled. He was allowed to play the tiger, though the actor Kenjirō still resented it, but he was not given any new roles. His fans were falling away, affected by the general prejudice against Koreans. Often he had to go away suddenly because Takayuki demanded it. He had a reputation for being unreliable and the theatre owner was fed up with him.

Kyu　　　　　But none of that matters now. I will be dead soon. I heard the tigers call my name in the streets of Seoul.

Sei　　　　　You have been in Seoul?

Kyu　　　　　That is the story I have come to tell you. You listened to me before and I believe you wrote everything down. You must write this down too.

Sei　　　　　Even if I write it down I don't suppose anyone will ever read it.

Kyu　　　　　One day it will come to light.

Sei　　　　　Well, I can only do my best. Go on.

Kyu　　　　　Takayuki is dead.

Tears formed in his eyes and slipped silently down his cheeks. For a moment I thought I was going to faint. The shock was even greater because the letter from Satoshi had raised my spirits so much.

Kyu　　　　　Takayuki is dead and I killed him.

Sei　　　　　In Seoul?

Kyu　　　　　Yes, right after he and the others murdered the Queen.

Sei　　　　　Queen Min was murdered? When? There've been no newspaper reports . . .

Kyu   The Japanese are trying to keep it quiet.

Sei   You cannot conceal the murder of a ruling monarch!

Kyu   You are right. Foreign journalists are reporting it already. But will anyone hear of it in Japan?

Sei   What happened? Were you there? And why? What can they have been thinking of? Whatever did they hope to achieve?

Kyu   I can only tell you about Takayuki's motives. He was there to avenge Kim Ok-gyun. You know Kim was lured to China and assassinated. Takayuki had sworn to Kim he would support him. He has been sending him money for years and encouraging him to believe one day Japan would back him with more than vague promises. He was horrified and enraged by the way Kim Ok-gyun died and what the Koreans did to his corpse.

The people he associates with, Black Ocean, have always held that the Korean problem would never be settled while the Queen lived. They saw an opportunity; the Foreign Minister, Inoue, resigned, and the new minister is more direct and more brutal. Takayuki was ordered to Korea and he asked me to go with him. He doesn't trust any other interpreters but I always tell him the truth. I am with him day and night. I hear and see everything.

Do you remember the kabuki performance for the Emperor? I was in black, at the side of the stage, watching Takayuki. You were there, I know. Did you see what I saw? Did you notice Takayuki's reaction when he set eyes on the Emperor for the first time? He recognised him.

Sei   So it is true?

Kyu   He was convinced the Emperor was really his brother. He discussed it with no one but me – not even Michi. In the end, when it counted, he was closer to me than he was to her. I thought it was a fantasy, a delusion. But on the way to Seoul, on the ship, one of the leaders of the Japanese assassins spoke to Takayuki in veiled terms, saying for all her faults the woman was a queen and it was only fitting it should be Takayuki who delivered her punishment.

Sei   That merely indicates they knew what he believed and were using him. Maybe the whole thing was an elaborate intrigue designed to enmesh him.

Kyu   I've also thought that way. There is a Japanese word for that, isn't there? *Kuromaku*, the black curtain, behind which unseen hands manipulate the action and arrange the scenery, just like I do in the theatre. None of us really knows who is running our lives. We play our roles like actors, as mindless and vain as a Sakutarō or a Kenjirō, conditioned to ignore the figures around us who are dressed in black and therefore invisible.

Anyway, Takayuki believed he was the Emperor's brother and it was his destiny to kill Queen Min. It happened in the women's palace. I can hardly bear to recall it but you must be told. Takayuki thought it would be a just execution but it was a shambles. Women's bodies naked are so defenceless, so pathetic. The soldiers abused them, hacked at them, urinated on them, groped their private parts and worse, and cut tufts off their pubic hair. Then they tried to burn them. Hundreds of Korean guards came and the Japanese ran away.

Takayuki was going to kill himself. I don't know if he had been ordered to or if it was the only way he could see to get

247

out of the whole disaster honourably. He knew before he left that he might not return for he told me what to do if he did not. At that instant he definitely wanted to die. It all happened so quickly. We had left the palace and were making our way to the river through the back streets. We saw the guards at the end of the alley. He thrust the sword into my hand and bared his throat to it. I didn't really do anything, just held the sword firm as he whipped his throat across it.

I shouted in Korean, 'This one's dead!' The guards ran on in pursuit of the others and I knelt by Takayuki as his life drained away. There was a lot of shouting in the distance but around us all was quiet. Dark and quiet. It was then I heard the tiger scream, calling my name.

I wanted to carry Takayuki's body back to the port but he was too heavy for me. I had to leave him there, with his sword. I should have brought that home for his son, but I had no way of concealing it. Now I am haunted by what they would have done to his corpse. And haunted by no one knowing what happened to him, which is why I came to you.

Sei   You have not told his wife? Doesn't she know he is dead?

Kyu   I am hoping you will tell her.

Sei   Me? Why me?

Kyu   If I go they will know, they will suspect I have told her everything and then her life will be in danger, and her son's.

Sei   Why should they be in danger? Your imagination is running wild. I can understand why, you have had a terrible experience but . . .

Kyu   Think about it. The Emperor has only one son, who everyone says is half-witted and sickly and no one ever sees. The boy who might be his nephew is intelligent and healthy. Black Ocean have their agents working in the house – you know the maid, the big woman?

Sei   I know her all too well.

Kyu   Takayuki had false identity papers made for Michi and the boy. He could not leave them in the house in case the maid found them. He gave them to me and I hid them away at Hirano's. I have them here, and some money. You must take them to Michi and tell her to leave Tokyo. She must go as far away as possible – not to her family home in Yamaguchi, but in the opposite direction, Hokkaido, Kushiro . . .

His gaze turned to Satoshi's letter, which lay on the floor between us. He took a small packet from his kimono and laid it down next to the letter.

Kyu   I hated her for years, you know. But at the same time I always looked on her as my older sister. I owed her a debt and now I am discharging it.

I<small>T WAS RAINING</small> heavily when Kyu left. I watched him walk away beneath the huge bat-like umbrella. Aka-chan came out from under the verandah, covered in cobwebs and whimpering. I patted him for a bit, then I went inside and read Satoshi's letter.

My dear Master,

It is getting colder here. The days are sunny with blue skies but there are already frosts at night. This morning Mount Rausu's peak was white for the first time since last winter. Snow can fall from a clear sky on the peaks. I did not know that and it always amazes me.

I wonder if you remember me at all. I recall with great pleasure the hours we spent together with Guy de Maupassant. Do you still tell the story of Roly Poly? I rarely have the opportunity to speak French now, other than to my cat, though occasionally a Russian sea captain whose acquaintance I have made arrives at the port and we converse in French.

Now I am free I am teaching children in a school run by one of the churches here. I enjoy it far more than I thought I would. I have become accustomed to Kushiro and I do not think I will ever return to Tokyo. I like this northern place with its huge skies, its snowy winters and its sense of adventure. I am slowly learning the Ainu language. They have many fascinating myths which one day I hope to tell you about, knowing your interest in all forms of story.

I miss my books. I am writing to ask you, if it is not too much trouble, to send them on to me. Please don't feel badly if you have sold them; it would be a small repayment for all your kindness to me.

Do you still see Dr Itasaki? I call her that as I imagine she is qualified by now. Please pass on my best regards to her.

Your old friend,
Okuda Satoshi

I showed the letter to Tae and she immediately began to dust the books and prepare them for packing, from time to time letting out little exclamations of incredulous joy, as though she had to keep repeating the news that Satoshi was alive in order to believe it.

I was having similar problems with disbelief. I wished I could confide in her. One moment I believed all Kyu had told me; the next I dismissed it as a wild invention. The following morning

I read the newspapers from beginning to end and found no mention of the attack in Seoul. I wondered if I should go to Michi and how I would break the news to her. I dreaded informing her that Takayuki had died and then finding it was not true, but at the same time I felt curiously guilty that I should know and she should not. I was also reluctant to go to Takayuki's house and front up to Aneki. Even though I looked several times inside the package at the money and the identity papers, I began to think I had imagined or dreamed the whole thing.

In short, all day I hesitated like an old man while my sense of foreboding deepened.

Tae   I don't understand why such good news should make you so gloomy!

Sei   I am just a little depressed.

Jack   Have a drop of whisky. That will raise your spirits.

Shigure   Are you struggling with one of your stories? That often makes me very despondent. The best thing I've found is to sleep on it. Problems have a miraculous way of solving themselves overnight.

Tae   You know you are getting old when your children's advice starts to sound sensible!

Shigure   I know you never expected it, Mother, but I actually am quite a successful novelist!

Tae   You are indeed. I might not say it very often but I am proud of you.

Jack   We all are. *Kampai!*

It was quite late that night when Kat'chan called at the door, waking Aka-chan and making him bark loudly in surprise. Shigure and Jack had already gone to bed, with the children, and Tae was waiting for me to stop sitting and brooding. She went to the door when she heard the dog bark, brought Kat'chan in, made him sit down and pressed a cup of hot tea into his hands. He was white and trembling.

Kat'chan   There's been an accident at the theatre. Kyu is dead. Somehow he was pierced during the tiger fight; he died instantly.

Tae   How terrible! What happened?

Kat'chan   No one's sure if it really was an accident or if Kenjirō killed him deliberately or if someone else substituted a real blade on the lance. It was one of those nights I've told you about when actors and audience fuse into a kind of enchantment and ghosts are released. Kenjirō seemed to be possessed by his role as Katō Kiyomasa. I've never seen him so powerful. And the tiger was completely real. He attacked it in a frenzy and it – Kyu – screamed in a voice that was part human and part from some other world. He fell to the ground, the set revolved on cue, Kyu did not get up, and we saw blood was flowing from beneath the costume.

Tae   Did you stop the play?

Kat'chan   You'll think I'm heartless but it was impossible to stop it. It had its own momentum. It rolled over us all. Kyu was dead – there was no way he could have been saved. I'd probably have had a riot on my hands if I'd tried to send the audience away, so I had the body moved to a dressing-room and let the play run to the end – the longest hours of my life. Then I sent for the police. The theatre will be closed for a day or two, then they will start a new play, but they'll have to do it without me.

Sei   You must not blame yourself.

Kat'chan   It's my responsibility – everything that happens while the play runs is. I can't do it anymore. This will be the end. I'll arrange the funeral, then I'm leaving – the theatre and Tokyo.

Tae   Where will he be buried?

Kat'chan   In Narita-san, I suppose, in the actors' cemetery there.

Sei   Poor Kyu. You know he was expecting to die soon?

Kat'chan   He told you that? When?

I described Kyu's visit briefly, not revealing all the details and not mentioning Takayuki's fate, just saying there had been some incident in Seoul and Kyu had heard a tiger call his name, which he was convinced heralded his death.

Kat'chan shivered.

Kat'chan   Was it a sort of suicide? I could tell the police that. That would be the least disruptive to the company. Perhaps he swapped the blade himself. Is that plausible?

Sei   It is the sort of dramatic gesture he would have chosen.

Tae mentioned Satoshi's letter and I took it out and showed it to Kat'chan. His expression lightened as he read it.

Kat'chan   I know this school! It was founded by my church as an outreach from their base in Hakodate. So our prayers were answered and Okuda Satoshi is teaching there? I've always wanted to visit it. Mount Rausu! I would love to climb that peak. Why don't I take Satoshi's books to him? Yes! As soon as I have settled Kyu's affairs I will go. I will see if it is a suitable place for Yuri and the boys to live permanently. What a clear message from God! He turns disaster into triumph and we are all in his hands.

Sei   He is truly a master storyteller! I will come with you, and see Satoshi again.

I had a longing to visit that northern land and learn its stories. And I would take Michi there and reunite her with Satoshi.

Now I HAD a plan for Michi but I feared I had left it too late. I cursed myself for my lack of resolution and my cowardice. I did not sleep all night and went to Takayuki's house first thing in the morning. The rain of the last few days had lessened to a drizzle and the air was raw and cold.

Aneki opened the door and gazed on me impassively.

Sei   I am sorry to trouble you so early but I need to speak to your mistress urgently.
Aneki   It is not possible. I will tell her you called. I expect you wanted to express your condolences.
Sei   Eh?
Aneki   My master passed away suddenly.
Sei   That is shocking news, but I came for a different purpose. May I ask what happened?

Aneki   He died abroad. We only heard yesterday – a sudden illness, we were told. My mistress is prostrate with grief and can see no one.

Her eyes searched my face as if she could read my mind.

Aneki   Don't interfere in matters that don't concern you, Master. Stick to your make-believe.

She closed the door in my face. I stood for a few moments staring at the wet garden and thinking about Yamagishi Takayuki and his strange and complex life, reflecting on what had happened behind those shuttered doors and allowing myself to feel the bittersweet pangs of grief for him and for Kyu, for lives cut short, for dreams unrealised.

The police concluded Kyu's death was suicide. The actors, led by Kenjirō, protested against his burial in their traditional cemetery and we held the funeral service in our local temple and placed the ashes under a stone pillar next to our son's. I felt in a way I had adopted him, even if only in death. I paid for the carving of his names, both Japanese and Korean. We kept the details private – there had been some lurid publicity about the incident and I did not want undesirable people to attend – but I sent a message to Michi expressing my sympathy for Takayuki's death and telling her about Kyu's funeral. She came to the graveyard, the only other mourner apart from my family.

Afterwards the others walked home and Michi and I talked
for a while in the temple's quiet garden beneath the huge ginkgo
trees which were spilling their golden leaves all around us.

Sei　　　　I was very sorry to hear of your husband's death.

Michi　　　　He had wanted to die for some time. A kind
of desperation had taken hold of him after Kim Ok-gyun's
death – and other things that he did not talk to me about.
There are many things I miss about him and I grieve for my
son who, like me, will never know his father, but I also feel a
kind of release. No doubt you think I am unfeeling – I have
had to learn to be. You were right when you said it would be
a prison. It has been and still is. That feeling of release is an
illusion. I am watched day and night. If I go out, as I did today,
I must leave my son behind, almost like a hostage. They know
I will never walk away from him. But why don't they just let
us go now? What purpose do we serve?

Sei　　　　Who do you mean by 'they'?

Michi　　　　The people who ran Takayuki's life, who told
him what to do, who provided a house and money and servants
who double as bodyguards. The people who run things from
behind the scenes, who operate us all, the men in black, the
invisible ones. I longed for my husband's death to set me free,
but I am no less a prisoner than when he was alive.

Sei　　　　Your husband left something for you. I believe
he wanted you to escape. Kyu gave me a packet he had been
keeping for you, to be given to you in the case of Takayuki's
death. Papers, money – so that you can start a new life.

Michi　　　　Takayuki did that?

Sei　　　　I have the packet at home. I also have a letter

from Satoshi. He is still in Kushiro, but he is a free man now, a teacher. I am going to surprise him with a visit before the weather gets too cold. My son-in-law is coming with me. We are taking Satoshi's books back to him. I think you should come with us. We will go north by train and take the steamer across to Kushiro. Meet us at Ueno. I will bring your papers.

I told her the hour and the day. She smiled for the first time and promised she would be there.

A ND SO, MY dear listeners, I bring you to my happy ending. Dreams have been crushed along the way, lives have been snuffed out but love has endured. A man and a woman fell in love over some lines of poetry and were lost to each other for years until chance or fate or some other master storyteller brought them together again.

So Michi will meet Kat'chan and me at Ueno station. How does she escape the watchful eye of Aneki? Let's say she poisons her, for she still has the bottle of arsenic she stole from Dr Kida. Or perhaps she makes her unwell with senna pods or some other ferocious laxative, for she was and will one day again be a doctor.

Her son, Masayuki, will be with her, rcd-eyed from crying but stoic in the way of samurai children. Kat'chan, who is used to boys, will raise his spirits with stories about bears and hunters, dark endless forests and snowy mountains, and Masayuki will fall asleep eventually as the train follows its narrow track to the deep north.

Kat'chan will warn us that if the weather is bad we will be delayed at Aomori, but a late autumn calm will quieten the ocean and the windless days will be filled with a soft golden light beneath a pale blue sky. The peak of Rausu will be hidden in haze when the steamer docks at Kushiro; the town buildings with their white clapboards and steeply pitched roofs will look foreign to our eyes, as though we have arrived in another country. We will think how tiny they look, children's toys scattered on the edge of the wilderness.

We will see marshland where sky and water merge into one and thousands of birds fill the air. We will see shaggy horses and black-and-white cows, maybe even sheep. There will be tall grey-eyed Russians and Ainu women with tattooed mouths. Within a few hours we will become accustomed to the stench of fish.

We will make our way to the church, where the pastor will be a friend of Kat'chan's, a middle-aged man from Tokyo who has been here for seven years. He will have a large family who will carry Masayuki off for some game and we will hear the boy laugh for the first time.

The pastor will know Satoshi well. 'Our teacher!' he will exclaim. 'He is a wonderful man; the children love him.'

He will show us the way to the school. Kat'chan will be carrying the box full of books. Satoshi will be outside chopping wood, late afternoon, the sun setting, the children gone for the day. He will be thinner, his hair streaked with grey, his fingers calloused and inky.

There will be a cat. It will be tabby and white. He will call it Charles and talk to it in French.

Viens, mon beau chat!

I will call his name. He will turn, holding up a hand against the sun. He will drop the axe and step towards us.

We will embrace. There will be no words, just tears glistening.

He will take us inside. There will be a kettle hissing on a tiled stove. He will unwrap the books, stroking them and greeting them like old friends.

He will not look at Michi.

The pastor, Kat'chan and I will leave.

Will they be able to surmount all that lies between them? The years of separation and imprisonment, anger, guilt and regret?

I believe they will.

He will open a book. He will read to her in French. She will take off her jacket and make tea. She will warm her hands over the stove and take his feet between them. It will be the second time she has touched him. This time she will say yes. The cat will purr.

She will never return to Tokyo. No one will ever find her, or her son who might or might not be the Emperor's nephew.

I will go home, my head full of new stories. Kat'chan, Yuri and Soji will move to Kushiro, where Kat'chan will preach the gospel and climb mountains. Fusao will refuse to leave the theatre where he will one day become stage manager. Teru will open her shop and make mufflers and scarves suitable for the Hokkaido winter. Jack and Shigure's children will grow up lovingly neglected and fine. My infuriating but beloved Tae and I will grow old. I will not go blind. There will be a little lapdog, a present from Jack, who will torment another dog called Aka. Our grandchildren will have children. There will be another little boy telling stories about mice and sparrows, another little girl acting out plays with her dolls.

History will roll over us with its narratives of blood and terror and cruelty, its dark secrets and its untold tales. Truth will be chopped into pieces, ground into dust, buried under the earth, but it will never be completely silenced; its stories of resurrection and redemption will still be heard.

And now I leave you in the capable hands of the next story.

Author's note

WHEN RESEARCHING THE background for this novel, set in 1884, I was inspired by the outburst of energy and creativity in all forms of writing and storytelling that took place when literature from Western sources met the Japanese tradition.

Early Meiji period novels used a form similar to a stage play for dialogue. Sei uses this same form to record conversations, and I have used it in the novel.

Sei's melodrama, 'The Silk Kimono', is perhaps a forerunner to the great Meiji melodrama, 'The Golden Demon' ('Konjiki Yasha'), by Ozaki Kōyō.

The inspiration for Jack Green came from the English storyteller, Henry Black.

Pages 2 and 13: Among Jack Green's stories are adaptions of 'Jason and the Argonauts', 'Medusa', *Oliver Twist*, *David Copperfield*, *Bleak House* and *A Tale of Two Cities*.

Page 12: *The Eight Dog Chronicles* by Kyokutei Bakin was a huge and immensely popular historical novel, which appeared in the first half of the nineteenth century.

If Sei had written 'I Am A Dog' he might have had the same success that Natsume Sōseki achieved with the satirical novel, *I Am A Cat*, written in 1905-6.

Page 16: Sei might perhaps be thinking of 'The Humble Man's Bobbin', an anonymous work about two Satsuma warriors that gained widespread circulation in the Meiji period.

Page 81: Satoshi's French novels are *Les Miserables* and *The Count of Monte Cristo*.

Page 82: The Baudelaire poem is 'L'Invitation au Voyage'; *Mon enfant, ma soeur, Songe à la douceur. D'aller là-bas vivre ensemble! Aimer à loisir, Aimer et mourir. Au pays qui te ressemble!* (Translated by LH.)

Pages 85 and 225: Shigure's stories are inspired by Higuchi Ichiyō and other Meiji women writers.

Page 116: The Guy De Maupassant stories are 'Boule de Suif' and 'Deux Amis'.

Page 181: 'Shibahama and The God of Death' can be found in Tatsumi Yoshiro's *Fallen Words*. Tensa's other tales are traditional *rakugo* tales. His final story is invented.

Page 195: 'The Little Sparrow' appears as 'The Sparrow's Gifts' in Royall Tyler's *Japanese Tales*.

Page 196: The old man's stories are based on tales from *Legends of Tono* by Kunio Yanagita.

Page 236: Jack Green's final stories are *Treasure Island*, *Robin Hood* and *Vice Versa*.

The kabuki plays, *Osaka Castle* and *Hideyoshi's Invasion*, are both invented, as is 'The History of a Nose'.

I would like to thank Randy Schadel, Carmen Sterba and Gay Lynch for reading the manuscript for me, and for their suggestions and corrections.

BLOSSOMS AND SHADOWS

Japan, 1857

For centuries Japan has been isolated from the rest of the world. But the Western powers are now at its shores, the government is crumbling and revolution is building. The samurai age is coming to an end and in its place a new Japan will be born.

Into this turmoil steps a young woman. Tsuru expects to marry a man of her parents' choice but her life is taken over by the beliefs of the time and by the passionate men around her. Their slogan is *Sonnōjōi* (revere the emperor, expel the foreigners), their preferred method is violence.

Blossoms and Shadows is a compelling and beautiful tale of love and war, women and men, and the rise of modern Japan.

'fascinating historical epic'
Sunday Telegraph

'all births are bloody and the characters in
this strong novel pay a high price for living
in interesting times.'
Sunday Age